THE HOUSE ALWAYS WINS

TOM MINDER

Black Rose Writing | Texas

ISBN: 978-1-68433-122-2
PUBLISHED BY BLACK ROSE WRITING
www.blackrosewriting.com

Printed in the United States of America
Suggested Retail Price (SRP) $17.95

The House Always Wins is printed in Gentium Basic

I'd like to thank Nick May from Typerightediting for fine tuning the narrative, and Dawn Byrne and Vicki Lees for their helpful beta feedback. Thanks also to The South Jersey Writers' Group, and The Writers' Coffeehouse for their continued guidance. Finally, thanks to my wife Paula, who has supported my dream.

The House Always Wins

CHAPTER 1

(Sunday Evening, the 12th)

LaVonne Wilson pulled the log book from her satchel and smiled at the *Hello Kitty* sticker waving back. She entered her position: third level parking, inner lane, facing the elevator atrium. She checked Mickey and made her entry:

Time: 10:45 p.m. Status: All Quiet.

She put the log away and continued to walk past the endless row of cars. *I wonder who's winning in Dirty Sam's tonight, and how many mortgage payments are being lost.*

Swinging her flashlight, she exposed the dark corners of her domain. Nobody lurking. *Good.* She stopped and moved the light to a Nissan about ten cars down: some poor guy, head pressed against the driver's side window, sleeping it off, no doubt. *I'll have to rouse him and send him on his way. The casino isn't running a flophouse.*

Tapping the end of the flashlight against the window, she shouted, "Hey buddy, wake up. Time to hit the road." No response. She leaned in and rapped with her knuckles. That's when she saw the blood splattered on the dashboard and the shattered windshield.

She shone the light on the man. "Oh, my God!" She fell to one knee and vomited the chicken noodle soup she had just eaten.

Catching her breath, she called her supervisor. She stood, using the door handle for support, and forced herself to look at the man. *That poor guy looks familiar. What's left of his face, anyway.*

Ten minutes later, a heavyset EMT spilled out of the ambulance, saw LaVonne, stuffed his overhanging shirt into his pants, seemed to check his breath, and walked toward the Nissan. "Hi LaVonne. How's my favorite member of law enforcement?"

"I'm not a cop, Ray. I've told you that. Just a guard doing her rounds." She nodded toward the car. "Here's the victim. Looks like he was shot at close range." She pointed to the concrete floor. "Watch out for the puke."

Ray sidestepped the puddle of mushy noodles, leaned forward, and looked into the front seat. "Wow. What a mess!" He called to his partner. "Hey Billy. No need for an IV. This guy's long gone."

• • • • •

LaVonne put down her coffee and pulled the blanket around herself as she sat in the small security office in the basement of Dirty Sam's Casino. Manny Gomez, her supervisor, sat next to her and rapped his fingers on the Formica desktop.

A young man in suit coat and tie entered the room, pulled out a metal chair across from them, dropped a notepad on the tabletop, and reached across the table. "I'm Ted Hanson, lead detective for the Long Harbor police." He waited for LaVonne to recognize the pleasantry. She pulled her arm from under the blanket and shook his hand.

LaVonne's watch pointed to one o'clock. "Hey, a Mickey Mouse watch. I haven't seen one in years."

"It was a gift from my dad," she said, forcing a smile.

"LaVonne's dad is Mayor Wilson," Manny said. She scowled at him. "But she's a damned good security guard in her own right. And we believe in diversity here at Lucky Roller Security."

They both stared at Manny. He slumped.

Ted sat, wiggled on the pleather to establish an ass groove, and leaned forward. "So LaVonne. Take a deep breath and tell me what happened."

She sobbed as she recounted finding the body, the cops arriving and pulling the man from the car with the help of the EMTs, and Manny leading her away to this dingy office.

A patrolman entered and whispered in Ted's ear. He nodded and had the officer wait outside. "Where have I heard that name before?"

"Miss Wilson, Mister Gomez. Do either of you know a Vincent Ferrante?"

●　　　●　　　●　　　●　　　●

(Monday the 13th)

Police Chief Mark Porfino crumpled the McDonald's bag. He found the nutrition web site and searched for 'The Big Breakfast with Hotcakes.'

"Hmmm, One thousand three hundred and fifty calories. Hot Chocolate, three hundred and sixty. Have to go for a light lunch. Maybe Taco Bell."

"Sir?" Ted Hanson stood in the doorway.

"Oh, nothing Ted. Just going over my food choices." He stood, tucked in his shirt and pirouetted. "Funny, I feel thinner but the pounds aren't coming off. My wife's after me to eat better."

"You have syrup on your shirt, Boss. Remember to cover up the evidence."

Mark laughed, poured water on a few of the napkins in front of him, swiped at the stain, and checked himself in the window. "Seems to be gone." He waved to a chair. "What's up, Ted?"

The detective sat. "Does the name Vincent Ferrante sound familiar?"

Mark studied the ceiling. "Vincent Ferrante... Wait a minute. He was Mario Gallante's henchman who came to town when we were looking into Silvio Fortunato's death."

Ted sat forward. "That's right. I thought I remembered the name. Well, he was found dead last night in Dirty Sam's Casino. In the parking garage. Had a bullet through his head."

Mark took a sip from his hot chocolate and sat back. Ted gestured to his lip. The chief dabbed his face, saw the chocolate impression on the napkin, and laughed. "I guess there's always a piece of evidence that remains. Thanks, Ted."

"We're checking the surveillance camera now," Ted said. "So far, nothing showing the shooting. We do have a few shots of Ferrante before he got to his car." He pulled out a photo. "Here he is kissing a woman who appears to be wearing a waitress uniform. This is before he entered the garage. She looks familiar too."

Mark took the picture, studied Vincent, then the woman. "Well, I'll be. Carla Ciccone."

"Isn't she in Cambria?" Ted said. "Serving a sentence for manslaughter."

"She got out last year. I testified at the parole hearing on her behalf." Mark belched and tasted partially digested sausage. "This is starting to be a bad day."

•   •   •   •   •

Ted fast-forwarded through the surveillance tape. Two men talked near Vincent's car. The taller one had a heavy beard, which seemed to reach from chin to forehead. He offered a hairy hand and shook the offered limb of the shorter, clean-shaven man. Ted stopped the tape and zoomed in. "Well I'll be. Jim Cooper."

He viewed the taller man. Must be seven foot tall. Makes Cooper look like a midget. He started the recording again. The men turned toward Vincent's car. The hairy giant walked over, ripped open the gas lid, removed the cap and—oh God—pissed into the tank. Jim laughed at first, then called over to his friend. The man zipped, put his arm around Jim's shoulder, then the men walked out of view.

Thirty minutes later, Vincent unlocked his twelve-year-old Nissan. He seemed to sniff the air as he climbed in and turned the ignition. After a minute, he got out, popped the hood, and scratched his head. He returned to the front seat and tried to start the car again. He slammed the steering wheel, got out, pulled his cell, and made a call. After a minute, he put his phone away, mouthed an obvious f-bomb, and walked back to the casino elevator.

A tow truck pulled up next to Vincent's car minutes later. The driver jumped out and shouted, probably for Vincent. He waited a few minutes, then drove away. Vincent returned to the garage holding a Starbucks cup as the truck was leaving the parking level. He waved his free arm, standing on his tippy toes. Too late. He climbed into his car, tried again to start it, and stared forward after a few failed attempts. His head slumped to the side window as the windshield glass shattered. Twenty-seven minutes later, LaVonne Wilson tapped on the window to rouse the dead man.

•   •   •   •   •

Mario Gallante molded the Burger King wrapper, leaned back, and sent a skyhook of greasy paper toward the trash. The ball ricocheted off the wall and landed in the can. He gave himself a high-five, almost falling from the rolling chair. He crabwalked back to his massive desk. Picking up his 32-ounce coffee, he took a long sip, added yet more sugar, and searched for the morning edition of the Cambria Journal. Spotting it in his rarely used IN basket, he flipped past the national and local news sections and made a beeline for the Comics.

He began his daily assault on the Jumble, solved three of the word challenges, then struggled over R-U-D-M-R-E. He chewed the pencil.

"Ah, MURDER," he shouted.

His assistant, stood in the doorway. "Are you okay, Boss?"

"Irene, your fearless leader is not only a trick-shot artist, but a solver of life's mysteries. Those Jumble folks can't fool me."

She gave a thumbs up and walked back to her desk. Mario turned to the Local News section, glanced at the obituaries, then returned to the front page to catch up on Cambria and Long Harbor comings and goings. Above the crease was a photo of a lifeless man being removed by police from a car. Mario leaned forward, flipped on his desk light, removed a magnifying glass from the drawer, and examined the picture. "Hey, that looks like Vincent." He sat back. "Irene, get in here, now."

Mario held up the paper as she hurried in. "Who does this look like?"

She put on her reading glasses and studied the picture. "It looks like Vincent." She mouthed the caption. "The name of the victim has not yet been released pending notification of next of kin."

"I'm the closest thing he has to kin," said Mario. "Get me Chief Porfino from the Long Harbor Police on the phone."

•　　　•　　　•　　　•　　　•

Mark struggled over the Sudoku as his phone rang. He pressed the Speaker button. "Chief Porfino."

"Hello. This is Irene Foster from Gallante Plumbing and Supplies. I have a call from Mister Gallante. Are you free?"

Mario. Must be about Vincent Ferrante. "Yes. Put him on."

"Chief Porfino, how are things in lovely Long Harbor?"

"A bit busy, Mario. We have a murder in Dirty Sam's we're investigating. Looks like a crime hit. Know anything about it?"

Mario grunted. "No, Mark." He lowered his voice. "Looks like it may be one of my plumbers, Vincent Ferrante."

"Did you send him to Long Harbor on business? Maybe he met someone who didn't like his line of work." Mark smiled. "Maybe he did a lousy job on a leaky faucet."

Mario checked the clock. "Look, Mark. I'll drive in later today to identify him and see what's going on." He snorted. "It will be like old times."

"Okay, Mario. Ted Hanson's lead detective on this. Let's all have a chat. Around three?"

"Yeah. Let's have a late lunch at Sheila's Diner."

"Are you sure Sheila won't spit in your beef stew? You did dump her for that blond stripper."

"I'll take my chances, Mark. See you later."

●   ●   ●   ●   ●

Ted knocked on Mark's door as he was hanging up. Mark waved him in. "Take a load off, Ted. I just spoke to Mario Gallante."

"I guess he figured out it was Vincent we pulled from the car." Ted sighed. "Ten years after Silvio Fortunato's death, and we're knee-deep with Mario again."

"He's coming to town to identify the body and look into the death," Mark said, shaking his head. "It *really is* déjà vu. We're all meeting for lunch at Sheila's...at three."

Ted sat up. "Man, the guy has guts. Sheila still isn't over his skipping out on her to bang that stripper."

Mark nodded. "Maybe we should order something different than Mario. Just in case." He opened his laptop and searched for the case status. "Did you get anything from the security cameras?"

"I did see two men near Vincent's car before he was killed. One was a tall, hairy guy in a Hawaiian shirt. Get this. He pissed into Vincent's gas tank."

Ted grinned. "Guess who the other guy was?"

Mark stared at Ted as the detective awaited a guess. "Who...dammit?"

Ted sat back, "Jim Cooper."

• • • • •

Jim Cooper returned home, dropped his lecture notes on the table, pulled his wallet, and examined the contents. *Man, 300 bucks up in smoke. I wonder how Herb can win at blackjack so consistently.* Brakes squealed in the driveway.

He sat at the dining room table, found a pen, and wrote gibberish on his presentation about environmental challenges facing Long Harbor. The front door opened. A leg, then a hand holding keys, and finally, a bag of groceries with an arm clutching them, came into view. Jim jumped and rushed over in time to catch the sliding bag before a clump of grapes could topple out.

"Thanks, Jim." She looked around. "Where's Mary Ann?"

Crap. I forgot to pick up Mary Ann. "Still at Janie's. I just got home from school. I'll pick her up."

Jan saw the crinkle in his forehead that indicated he was lying, and frowned. "Have you been to the casino again? I called your office, they said you left earlier in the day."

"I stopped by for an hour or so. Saw Herb there and we got talking. What a strange guy. Head to toe hair, but a real charmer with the ladies."

"How much did you lose, Professor James Cooper?" she said, her voice rising.

Shit. The full name. "I lost three hundred. I was ahead for a while and got cocky. Herb won five hundred. How does he do it?"

"Three hundred! I've warned you, Jim. Stay away from Dirty Sam's. You know you've got a gambling problem and we can't afford to lose a couple hundred a week on your habit."

She bared her teeth. "And lose your friend. He's bad news." She started emptying the bag. "Now pick up our daughter."

• • • • •

Sheila Jackson put down her coffee, swiveled on the counter stool, and scanned her restaurant, *Sheila's Diner*. She smiled. *Pretty full today. It took a few years, but now I'm making a profit, and getting good YELP reviews. People really love this place.*

The cowbell over the door clanged as new patrons arrived: Chief Porfino and Detective Hanson. She pulled two hefty menus and smiled to the men. "Mark and Ted. Welcome. Here for a late lunch?"

"Of course, Sheila," Mark said. "An army travels on its stomach. What's today's special?"

"We have meatloaf with mashed potatoes. That'll stick to your ribs." She waved towards a chalkboard. "We also have a nice beef stew."

Mark smiled. "They both sound great." No Mario in sight. "We're meeting someone. We'll need a table for three, near the back."

Mark and Ted sat, examined the menu, ordered diet cokes, and awaited their guest. The cowbell clanged. Sheila picked up a menu and walked up to Mario. "Where's your floozy, you creep?" she said as she jabbed a finger in his chest.

Mario stepped back, grabbing the coat rack for balance. "Whoa, Sheila. Calm down now. She left me for a Texas Hold'em player. Last I heard, they were in Reno." He straightened his coat. "I'm meeting some friends for lunch."

He saw Mark and Ted and waved. "There they are, just like old times."

Sheila swatted Mario with a menu. "Seat yourself." She smiled. "Try the beef stew."

Mario carried the menu and took the walk of shame as patrons whispered, then looked down when he made eye contact. He slid into the booth next to Ted, dropped the menu on top of a placemat advertising Dirty Sam's, and signaled for the waitress. "I'll have exactly the same thing they're having."

Mayor Evers Wilson and LaVonne walked in and nodded to Sheila. "Mayor Wilson, how are you today? And LaVonne." She took a full body scan. "You get more beautiful every day, young lady." LaVonne blushed and mumbled a thanks. They followed Sheila down the long aisle. Evers smiled and waved to each constituent, shaking any hand not holding a fork.

Mario glanced up from his bean soup. "Hey there's your black, Republican mayor." He watched the man approach. "I can see the charm people talk about."

Evers stopped at the table. "Chief Porfino, and Detective Hanson." The men dropped their napkins and started to stand. "Please, don't get up." He towered over Mario and offered a hand. "I don't believe we've met. I'm Mayor Wilson."

Mario took his hand while standing. "A pleasure to meet you, Mayor. I'm Mario Gallante, from Gallante Plumbing and Supplies in Cambria." The handshake continued until Mario loosened his grip. "I've heard a lot about you, Mayor: retired marine captain, Iraqi vet, master politician."

The three men stared at LaVonne. "Oh, where are my manners?" said Evers. "This is my daughter, LaVonne." Mark, Mario, and Ted stood as Ted said, "We've met. Hello again, LaVonne. This is Mark Porfino, chief of police, and Mario Gallante." He turned towards the men. "LaVonne discovered Vincent last night. She's a security guard at Dirty Sam's."

Ted turned to Mayor Evers. "Mayor, Mario is Vincent's employer. He's here to identify the body."

Mario nodded to Evers and LaVonne. "And to provide any help I can offer."

LaVonne nodded. "I still see that poor man slumped over. What makes someone do that?"

Evers shrugged, then spotted Sheila. "Oh, there's our hostess. Is she stamping her foot? Must not get on her bad side. Enjoy your lunch, gentlemen."

The waitress arrived with the meatloaf. Three identical orders. She placed the entrees before the men. Mario looked over to Sheila, who smiled. He switched plates with Ted. "Just in case," he said. Sheila grinned and greeted new guests.

Mark cut into the ground beef and took a taste. "Ah, this is good." He smiled at Mario. "And no bodily fluids from what I can tell."

Mario dug in. "Hey, this *is* pretty good. I guess Sheila isn't sabotaging the bill of fare. That's a relief." He took a sip of his diet coke. "Nothing unusual there either."

Mark dabbed his mouth. "So, Mario. You're in town to identify Vincent."

"Yeah, that, and to conduct other business. Must check on my Long Harbor plumbing affiliate. I'll be staying at the Days Inn for a few days." He broke open a roll. "I'll identify Vincent tomorrow morning. He's not going anywhere right away, I assume."

Ted signaled for a refill of his drink, then turned to Mario. "I have to say, you seem pretty callous about this. You lost a long time employee, and, I assume, friend."

Mario shrugged. "A longtime employee, yes. A friend, ummm." He sopped his cheesy bread in the brown gravy. "Vincent has always been a tough nut to figure out. A reliable worker who carried out his assignments efficiently, but I never completely trusted him. It always seemed like his loyalties were elsewhere."

•   •   •   •   •

The apartment manager, Mrs. Harding, unlocked the door to Vincent's Long Harbor flat. Mark and Ted followed as she switched on the lights. The men walked through the common area, the bedroom, bath, kitchen, and finally out to the balcony. "Well, Vincent kept a tidy apartment. Not flashy, but functional," Mark said.

"And a rather pedestrian view of the city. No harbor view, just a place to hang your hat."

They reentered the living area, leaving the balcony door open to allow the breeze to enter the small unit. "Hey," Ted said. He walked over to a corner lit by a small lamp. "Vincent had a goldfish."

"He loved that fish," Mrs. Harding called out. "Called it Leona. Said he named it after his aunt."

Mark leaned over and put his face an inch from the tank. "Poor little gal. Your master's gone away." He smiled. "Believe it or not, Ted, we used to eat these on a dare at college."

"What do goldfish taste like?"

"I could never tell. Down the hatch, then chase it with a Bud."

Mark turned to Mrs. Harding. "We'll need about an hour here. We'll let you know when we're done."

Mark went to the desk next to the fish bowl and opened a laptop sitting on top. Goldfish wallpaper. He pressed the Enter button. A password prompt. He typed "Leona," and the screen came to life.

He opened the email app. A prompt for user name and password. He entered "Vincent," then "Leona." No luck. Hmmm. *I can only try three times before it locks me out. Better get the police cyber guys to look at this.* He found MS Word, and selected a file named "Layout." It opened to a drawing. *This looks like some sort of blueprint. Maybe a parking lot. No, I see support pillars. A parking garage. Hey, that could be Dirty Sam's.*

"Hey, Ted."

His detective came out of the bedroom holding a blue box. "Condoms, Mark. Only a few left. I guess he kept busy."

'We'll have to ask Mrs. Harding who she's seen in and out with Vincent." He nodded to the screen. "What's that look like?"

Ted leaned closer. "Well. I'll be, Dirty Sam's garage." He pointed to an area near the elevator. "This is near where Vincent was shot."

"What else is in the drawing? He couldn't have forecasted his death."

Ted scratched his chin as he took in the details. "Well, the elevators, the security door…"

Mark leaned closer. "Hmmm, the security door. Isn't that where the Brinks truck loads the casino proceeds? Twice a day at 5 p.m. and midnight is what I hear."

"You think he was planning to rob Dirty Sam's?"

Mark tapped the desk. "Possibly. Not by himself, I would think. Maybe he was working with someone. Someone who could do the planning while Vincent did the heavy lifting."

CHAPTER 2

(Tuesday the 14th)

Herb Pine rapped his knuckles on the table. The dealer slid a king in front of him, joining the six and the three. "I'll hold." After completing the hands of the other gamblers, the dealer turned his hold card exposing a seven, next to his five. He pulled a card. "A Queen. Dealer busts."

He slid chips to each winner, matching the bet of those who hadn't gone over 21 themselves. Herb took the two $100 chips and placed them atop his pile. He took a quick calculation. *Up two grand, I better cash out. Besides, I'm hungry.*

Tossing a $50 chip to the dealer, he dropped the rest into his pocket, waved to the remaining players, and headed toward the restaurant. The cashier looked up from the register and smiled. "Mister Pine, ready for some breakfast? We have a nice Eggs Benedict today, a honey-cured ham, and of course, a nice Mimosa with freshly squeezed oranges."

"No squirrel today, Mandy?"

She laughed. "You and your nature jokes. No, I'm sorry. And no possum today, either."

"Pity," Herb said. "They really spice up an omelet."

She led him to a corner table and signaled to a waitress. "Elley will serve you today."

"Where's Carla? She's my favorite."

"Didn't you hear? Her boyfriend was shot Sunday night, right in the parking garage. Apparently, half his head was blown off." Herb was silent. "Oh, well," said Mandy. "Enjoy your breakfast."

Herb opened his cell, and scrolled to The Long Harbor Press icon. He opened the app and selected the local news.

"Ahem."

Herb looked up. "I'm Ted Hanson from the Long Harbor police department," he said as the waitress placed a Mimosa in front of Herb. "Just orange juice and coffee for me," he said to her. "Hmmm. And maybe a bagel with cream cheese." He pulled the chair across from Herb. "Mind if I join you for breakfast?"

•　　　•　　　•　　　•　　　•

Carla Ciccone walked into the Long Harbor police station and asked for Mark. She sat while the desk officer called the Chief. "Okay, I'll bring her down," he said, and hung up. "Miss Ciccone, if you can follow me." She wobbled on standing and grabbed the arm of the bench to steady herself. The patrolman hurried over. "Are you ok, ma'am?"

Carla nodded, but gripped his shoulder. "Let me bring you to the visitors lounge. I'll have Chief Porfino come down." He waved to a female officer. "Can you help Miss Ciccone to the lounge?" He called Mark and explained what happened.

Carla was leaning back on the couch, eyes closed. She sat up when she heard Mark come in. He walked to the water cooler, half-filled two Styrofoam cups, and sat next to her, handing her one. "Drink this." She complied.

Mark opened a flask and poured bourbon into the second cup.

"Now drink this."

Carla emptied the cup, leaned back, and sighed. Mark handed her the flask. She took a healthy swig, wiped the mouth as a courtesy, and offered it back. "No, I'm good," Mark said, waving her off. She fastened the cap and slipped it into her purse.

"So, Carla, I'm guessing this is about Vincent."

She pulled a Kleenex and honked loud enough so that those walking by stopped short. Mark took the crumpled tissue and tossed it in the can near the cooler, as Carla wiped her hand on her pants. "I spoke with him a few minutes before he was killed. I said management suspected him of counting cards. He laughed and said it was a smokescreen, that he had bigger things in mind."

"Ok, let's take a step back. The last time I saw you was at the parole hearing. You were going to live with your sister when you got out."

"I did." She sighed. "But you know brothers and sisters, they don't always see things the same way. Sometimes all they do is get each other in trouble."

Mark sighed. "True enough, Carla. So how did you end up at Dirty Sam's?"

"My one and only skill is waiting tables. My old job at The Wharf brought back too many bad memories, and Sheila's is filled with people who knew Silvio. I wanted a clean break. Dirty Sam's opened, I got a Sheriff's card vouching for my good conduct after prison, took the training, fit into the skimpy uniform, and there I was."

"You met Vincent there?"

"Yes, quite a tipper, and a handsome, mysterious guy. We started dating, and he told me he worked on a contract basis, his little joke, for Mario at Gallante Plumbing." She laughed. "Small world, huh?"

"Did Vincent have any enemies? Anyone he was concerned about?"

"He kept things to himself. Like I said, mysterious." She frowned. "Actually, he didn't care much for Mario, and said Mario didn't care much for him."

Mark sat back. "Mario's in town looking into Vincent's death."

"Wow," she said. "What do they call that, déjà vu?"

"Yeah. We're all back on the roller coaster."

•   •   •   •   •

Carla returned to her apartment and searched for her black dress, last worn at Silvio Fortunato's funeral 10 years ago. She tried it on. *Still fits after all these years.* Looking in the mirror, she remembered that day. An emotional funeral mass, the long drive to Holy Innocents cemetery, standing in the back row with Gabe Cooper, Mark Porfino, and Ted Hanson, while Father Jim Cooper recited the last rites, then pointing her semi-automatic at Tony Wagner and avenging Silvio's death.

"And, after eight years in Cambria Correctional, I remade my life," she whispered. "A good job, a decent apartment, and a boyfriend until some snake shot him."

And here she was again, preparing for a funeral. No one to shoot this time. At least not yet. She slid the dress off, then put on her uniform for her shift at Dirty Sam's. Checking herself in the bathroom mirror, she saw Vincent's toothbrush, laying ready for the next use. She picked it up, rinsed it off as a last measure of respect, and dropped it into her trash can. "No more men for me," she mumbled. "Maybe it's time for a cat."

•   •   •   •   •

Herb poured ketchup on his Eggs Benedict, added pepper, and shoveled one muffin's worth into the opening in his face below the large nose and above the hairy shrubbery on his chin. As he chewed, he made noises not heard in nature. Ted opened his notepad. "Now, Mr. Pine," he started.

The man raised one finger, and waved it back and forth. Ted closed his notes and sat back. Herb smiled, showing a yellow mass covering his teeth. He swallowed, let out a Hollandaise-smelling *aaaahhhh*, and reached for the Mimosa. He emptied the glass in one series of disturbing gulps, swung his tongue around his teeth to dislodge any egg or muffin clinging on, then patted his mouth with the linen napkin.

"On Sunday night," Ted continued. Another finger. Herb dragged his coffee cup in front of him, poured in several sugar packets, stirred, and downed the hot liquid in seconds.

The neighboring male diners gasped as the females sat stunned. That is, those not taking photos and posting on Facebook. Herb nodded to Ted. The detective took a sip of his coffee, gasped at how hot it was, and dabbed his mouth to avoid spitting most of it out.

He brushed wayward coffee from his page, clicked his ballpoint, and looked up at the smiling man. "You were seen Sunday night near the Nissan driven by a Vincent Ferrante." Herb signaled for another drink.

"In fact, you were seen urinating into his gas tank." A woman at the next table spat out her orange juice as her male companion laughed. Ted turned to Herb. "And you were talking to an esteemed member of the community." The couple leaned closer. Ted pulled his badge. "Police business folks. Any chance you can visit the buffet table for a few minutes?"

They stood and headed for the omelet station. "Former Father Jim Cooper, Mister Pine. Now, I believe, a faculty member at Cambria Community College."

Herb picked up the delivered drink, took a civilized sip, sat back and smiled. "Jim's a casino buddy. A lousy Blackjack player, but an all right guy." He took a short pull from his refilled coffee and dabbed his mouth. "We knew Mister Ferrante from Blackjack. He was counting cards. Not real obvious, but I could tell. We were all heading to the parking elevators at the same time, so Jim and I were going to tell him to knock it off." Herb eyed the second Benedict portion. "But his girlfriend spotted him, came over, and pulled him aside."

Herb smiled. "I don't normally get intimidated, but the look she gave both of us scared the crap out of me. Jim must have had the willies too, because he said, "Let's go," and we went.

"I had seen the number on his parking level card, so we went up to three. He always parks near the elevator, so we checked for his car there. We found it, discussed what we would do next, and then agreed we should confront him next time. I needed to piss, so I decided to take care of nature and leave Vincent a message. Then Jim and I went our separate ways."

"And you went straight home?"

"After a quick visit to the all-night gentlemen's club on seventh." He reached into his pocket, and pulled a matchbook. "Birds of a Feather," Herb said, and laughed. "They weren't wearing many feathers Sunday night."

"How about Father Jim."

"I think he went straight home. I met his wife once. Not someone to be trifled with."

"So if I went to the club, they could vouch for you."

"Yeah. Tell them the Devil sent you."

●　　　●　　　●　　　●　　　●

Ted walked in, ordered a Diet Coke, and took in the surroundings. Men sat at tables drinking beer and enjoying the show.

"Hey, Teddy, remember me?"

He looked up at the stage. *Oh, God.* "Rhonda. I didn't know you worked here."

"I sure do, sweetie. Between escort gigs. Are you lonely tonight? I get off at six."

Ted slunk in his chair and glanced at his club mates. A lot of drunks. No one paying attention to the conversation since she could wrap herself around a pole while still talking. Ted pulled a five from his pocket and motioned her forward. She danced over and presented her G-string for an easy deposit. "Five bucks, Teddy. Are you looking for some one-on-one time?"

"I guess I am. But just to talk. When's your next break?"

"One o'clock. Are you sure you don't need any satisfaction?"

"I'll take a raincheck. I need to ask you a few questions." He smiled. "The Devil sent me."

•　　•　　•　　•　　•

Rhonda danced offstage, signaling Ted to follow. He walked into a dark room furnished with a small stained couch. She closed the curtain and signaled Ted to sit. He took out a pad, flipped to a blank page, and clicked his ballpoint. She walked over, crotch-level to his hands, pulled the notebook and pen from his grasp, and positioned herself on his lap. He started to talk but was muffled as she pulled his head into her chest.

"So, you're a friend of the Devil. He usually likes it slow and easy. How about you, Teddy?"

She reached inside his pants, found his control center, and started rubbing. Ted groaned, closed his eyes, and smiled. He removed her top in one quick motion and pulled her closer. Rhonda positioned herself so they could lie prone. After that, a furious removal of undergarments led to a closer and prolonged interrogation.

•　　•　　•　　•　　•

She ran Ted's MasterCard through her smartphone app, printed a receipt, and had him sign. "Leave a nice tip, Teddy. You got more for your money than most."

Ted calculated 25%, signed, found his pants, searched for his pad, and flipped to the blank page, which had become creased when the couple rolled on top of it. The pen was on the floor, having fared better than its companion. Ted composed himself while Rhonda dressed.

"So Rhonda, when was the last time you saw the Devil?"

She smiled. "He goes by Herb to his close friends." She examined the strobed ceiling as she pondered. "It was Sunday night, around ten. He had a good night at Dirty Sam's and was spreading the wealth." She finished buttoning his shirt, found his handcuffs, and stroked them. "Maybe you can tie me up with these next time." She laughed. "So I don't resist."

Ted blanked, then remembered why he was there. He brushed his shirt to smooth a wrinkle and allow himself to refocus. "So how did the Devil, sorry, Herb, seem that night? Was he nervous, preoccupied?"

She fastened her top. "Hmmmm. Nope. Just horny."

"Did he say anything about his evening at Dirty Sam's except for winning at blackjack?"

Rhonda pulled back her hair and worked on a ponytail. She giggled. "Oh, he said he pissed into someone's gas tank. Imagine that. That must have ruined the guy's night."

Ted stood and kissed her on the forehead. "The guy had a pretty bad night overall."

•　　•　　•　　•　　•

Mark opened his file cabinet and removed a new flask of Jim Beam from a brown bag. He unscrewed it, poured some into his coffee, and sipped. "Ah, nothing like a new bottle." He flopped into his chair and swiveled to face the window. Across the street, Mrs. Galley, the owner of Harbor Florists, was standing at a lunch cart, holding a long sandwich and applying catsup. She looked up, waved, and smiled. Mark lifted his cup in salute. "If only everyone was as carefree as her."

"Hi, Boss," Ted said. "Got a few minutes?"

Mark spun around and saw Ted beaming, but a bit disheveled. "Come in, Ted, You look like you've been through the wringer. Need to use my john to straighten up?"

"Thanks, Mark. I'll just be a minute." Ted hurried over, closed the door, and checked himself in the mirror. *Man, I need to be more careful. Can't grab a nooner then parade into headquarters like I just rolled out of bed.* He pulled several paper towels, wet them, and gave himself a once over.

He walked back into the office, sat, and opened his notebook, having to straighten the page again. "So I talked to Herb Pine at Dirty Sam's. Quite a character." Ted laughed. "Also the hairiest man I've ever met. I followed him into the restaurant. The hostess told him that Vincent had been killed. He seemed surprised."

He saw the Jim Beam flask on the edge of Mark's desk and nodded to it. "Mark. You may want to put that away." He leaned forward. "Mayor Wilson is really cracking the whip. No reason to have him come down on the PD."

"You're right, Ted." He stood, picked up the flask and filed it under J. "So continue with Herb Pine."

"He eats and drinks like an animal. Yet, he has this aura of class that disarms everyone."

"Like a cunning predator," Mark said.

"Exactly! I think he'd be just as comfortable stalking in the woods as he is in Dirty Sam's winning at the tables and attracting the ladies." Ted closed his notes. "But he has an alibi for the time of the killing. He was getting a lap dance at Birds of a Feather."

Mark sipped his coffee. "Let me guess. You checked this out." Ted reddened. "That explains the unbuttoned collar and the uneven tie." He poured the remains of his cup into the trash. "I think we both need to straighten up our acts...or at least be more discreet."

Mark turned to his laptop, entered his login, then his password of

"1234." He opened the case notes and studied the photo of Pine. "Wow, this guy *is* pretty scary. I'll visit him later. Focus on Father Jim for the moment."

"Will do. So how did it go with Carla?"

"She was pretty shaken up. Talk about unlucky in love. First, Silvio is killed, then Vincent Ferrante is shot. She's going back to Dirty Sam's today. Says she needs the money."

"Does she suspect anyone?"

Mark nodded. "She thinks Herb might be involved, maybe Jim Cooper, or even casino management. Tomorrow morning, go see Cooper. See what he knows."

He searched for Dirty Sam's Casino and printed the directions. "I'll talk to the casino management. See what they thought of Vincent Ferrante."

•　　　•　　　•　　　•　　　•

Leona Galley opened her front door and stepped aside, clutching her mail, as her tabby rushed to freedom. She walked in, dropped her keys into the porcelain tray on the hall table and flipped through the envelopes. "Junk, junk, junk," she said as she tossed each solicitation into the flowered wastebasket.

She studied a manila envelope addressed to her in smeared writing. *My left-handed nephew.* Pulling a letter opener from the drawer, she slit the top in a quick easy motion and dumped the contents: a picture with a yellow post-it attached. It read: 'IT'S HIM.'

Removing the sticky note, she examined the picture. "Well, well. It's Herb Pine," she muttered. "The skunk who ripped me off ten years ago in Baltimore. Good work, Vincent." She smiled at the hairy creature and whispered, "You don't short change The Red Dahlia. You'll get what's coming to you."

She returned to her front porch, holding the photo. She saw two newspapers embedded in the rose bush. *Well, that answers why I didn't see the paper these last few days. That damn paperboy, I'll give him a talking to.*

Ms. Spots, her calico, darted in almost knocking her over. Muttering an obscenity not normally reserved for felines, she opened yesterday's paper and scanned the front page, then found the Local News section. She put on her reading glasses dangling from her neck, and squinted at the photo on the first page. "Oh, my God, that's Vincent," she whispered. "Who could have done this?"

The photo of Herb Pine slipped to the floor. She picked it up and brushed cat hair from the front. "Herb Pine? Are you involved with this?"

She powered on her cell, selected the text message icon, and scrolled to Vincent's recent messages. One from a week ago read, "There's a girl I met. Carla Ciccone. Works at Dirty Sam's. I'll bring her over some time."

Leona remembered how surprised she was when she saw this message. Vincent's not a one woman man. She must be quite a girl. She found the Dirty Sam's number, dialed, and asked for Carla. The woman explained she was working a shift and couldn't come to the phone. "Now hear this, young lady. I'm her acquaintance, and I need to speak to her. Let her know I called. This is urgent."

"Will do, ma'am. Let me have your number."

"Don't you have caller ID, dingbat? Have her call me back on this number."

Leona ended the call, sat, and stared at her cell. "Call me, damn it." She walked to the TV and switched to her favorite afternoon show. "What would you do in a case like this, Dr. Phil?"

•   •   •   •   •

Carla went on her break and saw the post-it on her time card: *Call Leona Galley at 856-555-2374. Who is this,* she wondered. *Wait a minute. Vincent talked about his Aunt Leona. Apparently, a tough old bird living in*

Long Harbor. I wonder if that's her.

She fired up a Camel, pulled out a molded plastic chair and dialed. One ring, then "Hello. Is this Carla?"

"Yes it is. Is this Vincent's Aunt Leona?"

"Yes, dear, and I just saw the picture in the paper. What bastard would do such a thing?"

Silence.

"Oh, I'm sorry. That was rather abrupt. We both suffered a loss. Can we meet sometime soon? Maybe tomorrow in the Starbucks at Dirty Sam's?"

"Okay, Miss Galley. I have my dinner break at seven. Is that all right?"

"See you then, dearie."

CHAPTER 3

(Wednesday the 15th)

Leona walked into the Long Harbor Police headquarters. The desk officer recognized her and smiled. "Mrs. Galley, what brings you here?"

"Why, it's Gail, isn't it. Your mother always buys those daisies when they're in season. How is she?"

"Just fine, Mrs. Galley. What can we do for you today?"

"I'm here to identify my nephew, Vincent Ferrante. Poor boy was shot Sunday night. I would have been here yesterday morning, but I didn't see the news until the afternoon. That damn paperboy. He must aim for the rose bush."

Gail dialed the coroner. "I have a Mrs. Galley here, Doctor. She wants to identify the body of Vincent Ferrante." A pause. "Yes, the shooting victim from Sunday night."

"Oh," she said. "Ok, I will." She hung up. "Mrs. Galley, someone already identified the body, a Mr. Gallante, his employer."

Gail waved to another officer and asked her to cover the desk. "Let me take you downstairs to talk to Dr. Fuller."

The women entered the coroner area and met the doctor. "Mrs.

Galley. I'm sorry, we couldn't determine next of kin, and Mr. Gallante offered to identify Vincent. I can have you look at the body if you want."

"That's ok. I've seen a dead man before. Has his body been released for burial?"

"No. The investigation is ongoing." He lifted the phone. "Do you want to talk to Chief Porfino or Detective Hanson?"

"No, Doctor. Let me think this over. Do you know where this Mr. Gallante is?"

"He left the Day's Inn as an address in case we needed to follow up."

Leona nodded. "Maybe I'll talk to him personally and thank him for taking the time to do this."

●   ●   ●   ●   ●

Ted drove from his apartment to the Willows section of town. As he turned onto Longshore drive, a car backed out of 118. *Jim Cooper.* Ted slowed, then followed the tan Focus. *Must be going to his college job.*

Jim took the expressway southbound, away from Cambria Community. He pulled onto the Crabport exit and continued toward Dirty Sam's. Taking a sharp left before the casino entrance, he drove another mile, parked in front of a townhouse, walked to the entrance, and rang the bell. Rhonda answered and smiled at Jim. The ex-priest walked in as she kissed him on the cheek. The door closed.

●   ●   ●   ●   ●

Mark pulled into the Dirty Sam's garage, showed his badge to the Lucky Roller guard, telling him that he had a meeting with the manager. The guard pointed to a reserved parking spot, then walked him to the executive office area. The men entered a bright cube farm and headed toward the corner office. A smiling, muscular man hurried out. "Hi, I'm Larry Harkins, day manager of Dirty Sam's." He grabbed Mark's hand before he could resist, and pumped it until Mark could break free. A thin woman, around 30, stood in the doorway. Larry turned toward her. "This is Greta Robinson, the night manager." She nodded to Mark.

"We'll take it from here," Larry said as he waved the guard away. "Chief Porfino, come in and take a load off."

Mark walked into a large office overlooking the gaming floor. Larry waved him over to the window. "We can see them; they can't see us." He laughed. "You get some real characters down there. Card counters, perverts checking out the cocktail waitresses, blue-haired old ladies who shake their fist at the slots. It's a jungle down there."

"So you can see everything going on," Mark said. "Must be really interesting."

"We have security looking for anything irregular," Greta spoke up.

"Lucky Roller?" Mark asked.

"Not Lucky Roller. They patrol the garage. We have a crew of professionals with training in human behavior. What you and I might miss, they can spot and alert management."

"Anything unusual about Vincent Ferrante?"

"Looked like he was counting cards," Greta said. "Funny thing was that he would lose enough to make us wary of accusing him." She pulled a roll of mints from her pocket, took one, offered the rest to Larry and Mark, who declined, and put it back into her pocket. "I'm giving up smoking. Have to put something in my mouth."

Mark sat and opened his notepad. "So you knew Vincent on sight. What was special about him that made you notice? Looks like you get quite a few people through here."

Larry poured a cup of coffee and waved the pot to Mark, who declined. "He was a creature of habit," Larry said. "He sat at the same card table, parked almost in the same spot, hell, and he even ordered a Schlitz from the cocktail waitress every time he played. We look for repeat customers and their patterns."

"If he was counting cards, why did he make it a point to lose?"

Larry shrugged. "I always thought he was up to something else. I couldn't figure out what that was. He would look around, focus on this viewing window, and smile. Not a broad grin, just a—I don't know—I'd guess a smirk. Once, he seemed to mouth 'Hi.'"

Mark stood and pointed to the window. "Well, I'll be. Jim Cooper."

Larry turned and nodded. "Another blackjack player," he said. "Not a particularly good one." He smiled. "He might as well play the slots. He'll still lose, but it will take him longer."

As Jim searched for an open table, he saw Ted and lowered his head. A schoolboy caught playing hooky. The men talked, and Jim pointed to the food court. They filed out of view from their glassed-in audience.

"I don't know the new guy," said Larry.

"That's Ted Hanson," said Greta. "He's got a thing for Baccarat. Comes in a couple of nights a week." She turned toward Mark. "He's a detective. Maybe you know him."

•　　　•　　　•　　　•　　　•

Ted bought Jim an Orange Julius. He ordered a strawberry smoothie and pointed to a table.

"So, Father Jim," he started.

Jim waved his hand. "Just Jim Cooper now. Professor at Cambria Community."

Ted took a sip, had instant brain freeze, and rubbed between his eyes. He coughed, then sputtered, "So how come you're not standing at a chalk board teaching hungry students?"

"I don't have a class till one p.m. I was in the area, so I decided to stop for a few hands of blackjack."

"I followed you, Jim. You were meeting with Miss Rhonda

Gilmore. I know you're married. Did you drop your marriage vows, too, after leaving the priesthood?"

Jim took a short sip, and sighed. "She's been attending classes, trying to straighten out her life. She didn't want to spend her youth pole dancing and screwing losers. I've been counseling her." He brushed condensation from his cup. "She works at Birds of a Feather, a real seedy joint. Do you know the place?"

"I've heard of it."

•　　•　　•　　•　　•

Ted was satisfied, for now, that Jim knew nothing of Vincent's killing. His story matched Herb's, and what showed up on the video. The men went their separate ways: Jim to his afternoon class, Ted back to the station.

As Ted drove by the club, he saw Rhonda sitting on the back step, smoking a cigarette and checking her cell. He realized he was running a red light and jammed his brakes, stopping feet from an oncoming SUV. The driver swerved and laid into his horn. The red light camera flashed. *Crap.* He mouthed a "sorry" to the driver and pulled back behind the stop line. He turned to Rhonda. She smiled and waved.

•　　•　　•　　•　　•

Mark stuffed the chicken bones, fries packet, and empty butter pats into the Popeye's box. He eyed the trash can, but decided any toss would miss the target and leave the bones and paper scattered on the floor. He grabbed the greasy container, stood, and ambled across the room, licking his fingers along the way. Dropping the ex-chicken into the can, he wiped his hands on his sleeve, and returned to his desk.

Seeing crumbs covering his blotter, he swept them into his hand and considered another trip to the basket. He peeked into the doorway for human activity, then tossed this last evidence into an envelope, which he placed in his top drawer. He took a long slurp to empty his drink, emitted an *aaaahhhh,* and, remembering his attempt to conceal evidence, retrieved the crumb envelope, stuffed it into the empty cup, reattached the lid and put it to the side.

Ted walked by, head down. "Hey, Ted, come in. Let's talk."

His lead detective sighed, stepped in, and pulled out a chair. "Ted, while you're up, could you drop this into the trash?" Ted picked up the cup, saw a strange envelope inside, shrugged, and placed the drink into the trash next to the box.

"So, Ted. I stopped by Dirty Sam's today to talk to Larry Harkins and Greta Robinson, the day and night managers. We were people-watching out the viewing window when we saw you meet Jim Cooper, then lead him away. I didn't expect to see Jim there. Were you able to question him?"

"Yes, he was there to play a few hands of blackjack before going to his teaching job at Cambria Community." Ted shifted. "But before that, he stopped at Rhonda Gillmore's house. He was there for an hour."

"The stripper at Birds of a Feather?"

Ted nodded.

"So Jim is cheating on Jan?"

"He said he was *counseling* her," Ted said, making air quotes. "Trying to steer her away from the lowlifes at the club."

"Awkward," Mark said. "Did he know that you *see* her once in a while?" Mark made air quotes.

"He didn't seem to. Anyway, he looks clean with respect to Vincent, so I sent him on his way. I drove back to the station, got distracted, and went through a red light outside the strip joint. The red light camera caught me."

"Ouch. Oh well, official business. We can toss the ticket."

"I'll pay it, Mark. I think the gods are telling me to watch my step."

• • • • •

Mayor Wilson searched for Vincent Ferrante online. Not much there, a good thing for a suspected hit man. He searched for Gallante Plumbing and Supplies. A grinning Mario graced the Home page. He selected the Employees link and scrolled to Vincent, in Gallante t-shirt, holding a wrench. A disturbing grin there, like he'd be happier crashing it into a deadbeat, than using it to tighten a connection.

Back to the Home page. "Gallante Plumbing and Supplies. Your one-stop shop for parts and services. Let our master plumbers fix your nastiest problems." Evers smiled. *Maybe like a client who hasn't paid off his gambling debts.*

He left the page and searched for Herb. Nothing there. He opened Facebook. Any Herb Pine there? *Bingo.* The seven foot freak smiled from his profile picture. Last posted address was a P.O. Box in Forked River, New Jersey. No occupation listed.

"Why did you come to our little berg, Pine? The lure of the casino? Is this where you went after Baltimore?" he whispered. He selected "1" on his speed dial. "Hi, LaVonne. Let me know the next time you see Herb Pine."

• • • • •

Mark found the Dirty Sam's business card and called Larry Harkins. "Larry, this is Mark Porfino. Thanks again for allowing me to visit."

"Sure, Chief. Always willing to help the local police."

"Do you know a Herb Pine?"

A laugh on the end of the line. "Sure do, Mark. Everyone here knows him. A high roller, a ladies man, and a big tipper." He laughed. "And the hairiest man alive. Hair covering all exposed parts." A pause. "Hold on, Chief—Hey, Greta, Chief Porfino wants to know about Herb Pine. Want to pick up the horn?"

A click. "Greta here. Mark?"

"Yes."

"He just walked in. Maybe you want to stop by."

• • • • •

Mark walked the gaming floor and marveled at the bright lights and carnival atmosphere. He stood in front of a slot depicting a South American woman in thong and matching maracas. "You going to play this machine, fella, or stare at the boobs?" He turned. A seventyish woman with pink, blue, and yellow hair held a purse and a dangerous glare.

"No, ma'am," he said. "It's all yours."

She grunted, sat, opened her small bag, and placed a troll doll on top of the machine. She signaled the hostess. "A Kahlua for me, Missy. And don't be cheap with the vodka." Mark stared at the woman. "What do you want, young man. Do I have to get out my mace?"

Mark shook his head. "Have a nice day, ma'am. Good luck." The woman grunted and turned toward the slot.

He walked along the waxed path leading to the table games: craps, roulette, baccarat, blackjack. He approached the tables, seeing men, women, drinks, gambling chips, cigarettes, and hostesses in black outfits only technically legal. He heard a cheer and noticed a roulette table with patrons mobbed around a mountain of a man in a Hawaiian short-sleeved shirt, his arms covered by silky hair, which matched his beard.

Mark wedged his way closer, showing his ID to sway those who initially objected to the intrusion. Herb Pine placed 50 on red, 50 more on odd, and 50 on street (7, 8, or 9). The croupier tossed the ball into the rolling wheel. "Seven," he called out after the wheel stopped. He slid 6,500 in front of Herb. The man smiled, exposing his imposing canines. Mark shuddered at the sight, as bookend brunettes cooed at Herb.

"Herb Pine?" Mark said as he showed his badge.

The man smiled and scooped up his chips. He tossed a twenty to the croupier, and fifty each to his dates. "I'll see you in a few minutes, ladies. I need to converse with my new friend, Mark Porfino, the chief of police."

•   •   •   •   •

The men walked toward the food court. "Hey, Dirty Subs, I need a cheesesteak," Herb said. They walked to the counter as a girl in pigtails greeted them. "Welcome to Dirty Subs. We'll fill you up."

Herb studied the girl as she adjusted her name tag. "Evie, I'll have a large cheesesteak, wit'—" He smiled. "Oh, and make sure you use Cheese Whiz on that." He hummed. "And large fries—oops, dirty fries—and a large drink."

Evie entered the order and looked at Mark. "Are you two together?"

He nodded. "I'll have a Tuna Hoagie with provolone, and a large soda." Evie and Herb stood in silence. "Okay, and large dirty fries."

The bill came to $40. Mark pulled his debit card, surrendering it to Evie. He started to sign the receipt. "Leave a nice tip, Chief," Herb said. Mark grimaced, then added $10. "Nicely done." The men walked to the soda dispenser. Herb manipulated the flavors like Van Cliburn tickling the keys. His 64-ounce cup held an oddly-colored mixture. He took a sip. "Just right."

Mark filled his cup halfway with ice and pressed the Diet Coke. "Really, Chief?" Mark stopped, emptied out most of the ice, found the Dr. Pepper, and squished the liquid into his Dirty Rootin' Tootin' Sam cup. "That's better." Mark nodded toward the corner of the room and the men slalomed between tables.

After a feeding frenzy, which left a fraction of his sandwich surviving the original onslaught, Mark sat back, emitted a sincere *aaaahhhh* and waited for Herb to come up for air. Herb downed the cheesesteak with fried onions and Cheese Whiz, took a few seconds to breathe, then sucked on the large drink until it was empty. He smiled at Mark who sat with mouth open, and signaled to his own chin. "Chief, you missed a spot."

Mark dabbed his chin and removed tuna salad. He considered eating the morsel, but wiped it into the napkin instead. "So, Mister Pine. I haven't seen you in town before. What brings you to Long Harbor?"

Herb smiled, exposing his canines. "Dirty Sam's, Mark. Can I call you Mark? Call me Herb."

"Sure."

"This little gem is a real find. Away from the boardwalk, mostly locals and some visitors from Delaware and Maryland. No phonies here, just people looking for a quick shot at riches."

Mark slurped his drink. "Someone once said that gambling is a tax on the stupid. You don't seem stupid, Herb. Do you have a day job?"

He sat back. "I did once. Postal clerk," he said, stroking his beard. "They let me go. I kept freaking out the customers." Both men laughed.

"Anyway, now I roam the Jersey Pines, hunting, fishing, and enjoying nature." He waved toward the gaming hall. "And driving over to Dirty Sam's when I need money and a free meal. No better study of human nature than a casino, Mark. Predators, prey, those who have adapted and keep a low profile, those destined to be eaten."

He lifted his cup, said "Be right back," and returned with another 64 ounces of strange brew. "Take Jim Cooper, an interest for the moment, of your Detective Hanson. "Former priest, college professor, married man with a kid, yet, he can't stay away from here." He took a sip. "Jim doesn't realize that these places bleed you dry and destroy your life." He smiled. "Unless, you stack the odds in your favor. This isn't chance for me. It's a business."

"I hope you stay available for the next few days," Mark said. "I may need to chat with you again about Vincent Ferrante, Jim Cooper, and your comings and goings."

"Of course, Chief. Here's my card." It read:

HERB PINE
HUNTING AND TRACKING SERVICES

The men finished their meal. Herb emptied the tray into the receptacle and turned. His jaw dropped as Leona Galley and Carla walked by.

Mark studied Herb then turned toward the women. "Leona Galley and Carla Ciccone. Do you know them? Carla Ciccone was Vincent's girlfriend."

Herb took a breath. "Yeah. Carla works in the Gold Dust restaurant down the hall. I didn't expect to see her so soon after her boyfriend died."

"I think she needs the money," Mark said. He scratched his chin. "I didn't know she was friends with Mrs. Galley. Let's stop by and I'll introduce you.

"That's okay, Mark. I have to be on my way."

•   •   •   •   •

Evers pulled into a parking spot, called LaVonne on his cell, and arranged to meet her at the Gold Dust restaurant on her break. He entered the elevator area, pressed the down button, and waited. The door to the next elevator opened. Herb Pine stood inside behind an elderly couple. Evers hurried over and slid in behind the pair before the doors closed.

"I can't believe we got tickets to Barry Manilow," said the woman.

"And I won two hundred bucks," responded her husband. He noticed Evers. "Mayor, it's good to see you. Coming back from games of chance?"

"No. Meeting a friend for a late lunch."

"Oh, Mayor, you got on the *Up* elevator by mistake. You'll have to get off and go down to the Casino level."

Evers glanced at Herb, nodding. Herb sighed.

"You're right folks. I should have checked the lights first." He left at the next floor and held the door for Herb.

"Excuse me folks, I'm getting off here too," he said, sliding past the couple. The doors closed. "Where now, Evers?"

•　　　•　　　•　　　•　　　•

Leona sipped her Caramel Macchiato, wiped the whipped cream from her nose, and examined Carla. "You're a pretty young lady. Vincent had good taste." She sighed. "I wonder who could do such a terrible, brutal thing."

Carla shifted in her chair. "I'd like to know that myself." She fumbled with her tea, spilling some on the table. "Sorry, this is tough for me. This is the second time a boyfriend has been killed." She poured in a sugar packet. "For a small town, this place sure gets its share of crime."

"Who do you think could have done it? Did Vincent rub someone the wrong way?"

"Maybe. He was counting cards. Not a good thing to do in a casino." She pulled a Kleenex and honked, causing Leona to juggle her macchiato. "And he said he had bigger things in mind for Dirty Sam's. He never told me what they were."

Leona wiped the spilt liquid from her hand. "Do you know Herb Pine?"

Carla nodded. "He's quite a specimen. Big, hairy guy. Big teeth. Good tipper, too." She laughed. "He calls himself The Devil. Actually, the last time I saw Vincent he was talking to Herb and Jim Cooper." She started to cry. "An hour later, Vincent was dead."

•　　　•　　　•　　　•　　　•

Evers whispered "Men's room" to Herb and walked ahead, entering first. Herb spotted the security cameras, paused for a few seconds, then pushed the door and walked in. The mayor locked the door, walked to the sinks, and turned the water on to add more noise. "Now, Pine," he started.

Herb held up a finger, walked to a urinal, unzipped, and shivered. A steady splatter hit porcelain, and a steam rose between Herb and the plumbing. "Aaaahhhh," he gasped. "I'm glad you stopped me, Evers. I don't know if I could have made it home." He shook twice, and started to zip. "Wait a minute." He unzipped, shivered again, and produced another waterfall. He zipped. "All done."

Evers stepped aside as the giant lathered his hands, placed them under the water, and then rotated his hairy mitts under the blower. "These don't dry quickly," he said as he wiped his pants to speed the drying. "So, what's up, Evers?"

The mayor studied Herb's seven foot frame. "I thought we parted ways in Baltimore a good ten years ago. Now you're in Long Harbor." He leaned against a sink. "And, apparently, a person of interest in Ferrante's death. Can't you keep out of trouble?"

Herb brushed his shirt, and checked his hair in the mirror. "Look, Evers, Vincent's death surprised me too."

"Well, chew on this, my friend," Evers said. "I'm told he also was the nephew of Leona Galley." He smiled. "Remember her?"

"I saw her... shit!"

"Watch your hairy back."

Herb brushed his hair into place. "Did she ever find out we were doing surveillance on her? We probably stopped her from shooting up Baltimore."

Evers checked his tie. "I never actually met her there. I let Gladstone handle things. As I recall, though, you relieved her of fifty grand before you disappeared. You gave us enough info on her to cause us to look the other way." He straightened his cuffs. "She won't be as forgiving."

•   •   •   •   •

Evers left first and walked toward the food court. Herb waited a minute, then exited and turned toward the parking garage. He saw Jim Cooper's car approach. *Crap! He'll want to play Blackjack and chew the fat. I need time to think things over.* He pirouetted, and headed for the gaming area, hoping to duck out a different way. As he passed Starbucks, he saw Carla walking out, followed by Leona Galley. He lowered his head and continued forward. "There he is now," he heard. "Hey, Mister Pine."

He stopped, turned, and feigned surprise as Carla and Leona approached. "Carla, so sorry to hear about Vincent. Who could have done such a thing?"

Carla turned toward Leona Galley. "Leona, this is Herb Pine. A patron of the casino, and a gambling buddy of Vincent."

Leona offered a hand. Herb flinched, then shook. "Glad to meet you, Mister Pine. Leona Galley. Can I call you Herb? I'm Vincent's aunt." She let go of Herb and reached into her purse, pulling a black object.

She pointed it toward Herb as it emitted the theme to the Sopranos. "My cell, Mr. Pine. I love that theme. So catchy, and so New Jersey." She typed in her pin. "I'll let that go to voicemail. Let me check the lottery numbers, then we'll sit down together. Maybe we can figure out what happened."

•   •   •   •   •

Leona, Herb, and Carla walked to the gaming area. Carla hugged Leona and returned to her shift. When out of sight, Leona turned to Herb. "Feeling lucky, Pine?" she asked. "See that pair of Big Bang

Theory slots? Grab one and play a couple dollars a spin. I'll join you in a minute."

Herb nodded, sat at one of the two padded chairs, growled away a woman holding a glass of wine and eyeing the next seat, and started playing.

Leona walked in, stood next to the open slot, signaled the hostess, and ordered a gin and tonic. "Is this slot taken, young man?" Herb shook his head. She turned the chair so she could sit, then swiveled into playing position. She inserted a hundred-dollar bill. "Just the two of us. This will be comfy," she said, looking at the graphic display. "Those crazy nerds. How do they ever get laid?"

She patted his hand. "So, Herb. What are you doing in this one-horse town?" She selected a five-dollar spin and came up empty. "And more importantly, why did you skip out on me in Baltimore ten years ago?" She spun again, winning a dollar. "You owe me fifty grand, Pine." She spun again. "Plus penalties and interest. Let's call it an even hundred."

Herb spun and won $60. "You seem to be charmed, Pine." She cashed out. "I'm leaving now. You got till next week to come up with my money. Say next Wednesday. I'll give you till midnight." She stood and scanned the area. "Now where are those redemption machines?" She laughed. "Pine, you need some redemption yourself. A hundred grand should start the process."

The hostess arrived with the drink. Leona stood, downed the alcohol in a quick series of gulps, and handed her $20. "Here you are, Missy. And get my neighbor here a scotch on the rocks."

She turned to Herb. "Good luck, young man."

CHAPTER 4

Herb bet $5. No win. *Slot machines are a sucker's bet.* Taking the last sip from his scotch, he reflected on his day. *Mark Porfino, Evers Wilson, and Leona Galley, all giving me the third degree. And Leona, being a friend of Carla Ciccone, who was Ferrante's girlfriend. What else could go wrong? Maybe I should disappear into the woods until things blow over.*

No. Leona's on my scent now. The world's not big enough to hide from her for too long. I got away once. It's not likely I can do it again. Still, I need one more score to pay her back. Boy, look at the money passing hands in this place. I bet a hundred grand is chicken feed to them.

He glanced up at the glass partition. *Big brother has this place under a microscope. The only way for a quick payday is with help from the inside. Gotta keep a lower profile, though. Win some, lose some.* He smiled. *Well, I'll be damned. Vincent, you dog.*

Larry Harkins and Greta Robinson walked by. He picked up his glass and swirled an ice cube around his mouth. *There's LaVonne Wilson, Evers daughter and a security guard. There's a bunch of underpaid croupiers, cocktail waitresses, and plainclothes security goons. Who was in your corner, Vincent? Who was your inside guy?*

• • • • •

Larry entered the pin for the cashier door while Greta and a guard stood behind him, blocking any view of the code entry. The three headed to a back room where another pin gave access to the counting area. Cash sorting machines read denominations and routed each to a separate metal alley where the bills were bundled into stacks of one hundred each and given a Dirty Sam's band.

"How's the take today, Mike?" Larry said to the man overseeing the operation.

"Not bad, Larry. A typical weekday pull. Mostly slot money." He watched the bundles as they fell into a cloth sack. "The Brinks truck should be here soon."

Larry and Greta walked to a one-way mirror showing cashiers greeting clients, exchanging chips for currency, cashing slot credit slips, and supplying free vouchers to excited guests.

Ted Hanson stepped up and handed a check across the counter. The cashier smiled, examined his driver's license, placed the check into a slot, and opened the cash drawer. She counted out 10 one-hundred-dollar bills and slid them across. The detective nodded, slipped the cash into his pants pocket, turned, and seemed to look over the gaming area. He walked away toward the tables.

Larry looked at a security camera pointed at the tables. He followed Ted as the detective stood waiting for an empty seat at Baccarat. He found one, ordered a drink from a hostess, counted out some money, and waved the bills at the dealer. The man pushed the cash into a drawer, counted a pile of chips, and guided them across the table in front of him.

A blond in a low-cut red dress walked up to Ted, leaned in, and kissed his neck. He turned, smiled, kissed her, and handed her $200. Rhonda whispered in his ear and walked away, heading toward the blackjack tables.

•   •   •   •   •

Herb walked past the gaming tables on the way to the parking garage when he also saw Rhonda. She took money from a gambler and walked away. *Hey, I wonder who her date is.*

He sat at a slot a few rows from the gambler. The man turned to receive a drink from a hostess. *Well, I'll be damned. Ted Hanson. He must be banging Rhonda.* Herb put a twenty into the slot, Jungle Queen, waged it all and smiled at the odd pairing of detective and hooker. Five scantily dressed amazons slit into position, yielding a $10,000 win. Lights flashed accompanied by jungle drums announcing a new conqueror.

He sunk in his chair as other slot players and some table patrons watched the spectacle. He glanced up at Ted Hanson, who raised his drink in salute. Herb nodded as the attendant verified the result and counted out hundred-dollar bills until his prize total was reached. He thanked her, pocketed the cash, and stood to leave.

"Congratulations Mr. Pine," said Greta Robinson. "Today must be your lucky day." Larry Harkins walked over, holding a camera. Greta stood close to Herb, smiled, and discretely put her hand on his right ass cheek. "Smile Mr. Pine. Okay Larry." Larry frowned at Greta, then took the photo, blinding Herb by the flash. "Now sign this disclaimer, Mr. Pine," Greta said handing him a form, "and you'll be front page tomorrow."

Herb signed, bid Larry and Greta goodbye, and started again for the parking elevators. He looked over to Ted's table. No Ted. He spun around and saw him, arm-in-arm with Rhonda heading to the hotel elevators. *I guess we all got lucky tonight.*

He checked his cell for messages, bought a few lottery tickets, and took the elevator to his parking level. He mounted the Harley, pressed the starter, and put on his headphones. Adjusting the rearview, he saw a hand holding a gun. He ducked and felt a burning sensation as a bullet singed his beard and destroyed his windshield.

He pressed the panic button on his key chain. As the alarm blared, Herb slid off the cycle and looked back. No one there. He climbed back on, turned off the alarm, and sat in silence. A minute later, LaVonne Wilson tapped on his shoulder.

•   •   •   •   •

(Thursday the 16th)
The Law and Order ringtone woke Ted. Rhonda stirred at the noise, then went back to sleep. He sighed, and answered. "Ted Hanson." He listened to the patrol officer. "At Dirty Sam's? In the parking garage? When was this?" He checked the room clock: midnight. *Doesn't anyone get shot during daylight?*

"Yes, officer. I can be there in a fifteen minutes. McArthur Drive has an accident and is backed up? Thanks. I'll go another way." He left the bed, put on the clothes he wore hours ago, and checked in the mirror. *Not too ragged, I guess.* He found orange juice, and salted cashews in the minibar. As he ate his breakfast, he planned his arrival. He took the parking elevator to the fourth floor, found his car, checked in the mirror again, and pulled out. Heading to the third floor, he turned on his siren as he approached the level.

Flashing lights from two patrol cars framed a Harley. Glass was scattered. A man in a Hawaiian shirt stood next to one officer. *Herb Pine, how about that.* Ted pulled up, stepped out and approached an officer. "Detective, you made good time," the officer said. He turned toward the cycle. "A bullet was fired from behind, grazed the victim, and shattered the windshield. Lucky for him, he saw the gun in the rearview and ducked."

"Did you find the bullet?"

"Yes, it was lodged in the wall. We're digging it out now."

He led Ted to the victim. "Detective Hanson. This is Herb Pine."

Ted nodded. "We're acquainted, Officer. I'll take it from here. Gather any evidence, and get a match on the bullet." The officer left and joined his partner digging into the wall.

"You did make good time this morning, Detective," said Herb grinning. "I guess not too much traffic after midnight."

Ted frowned. "So, Herb. Who wants you dead?"

•　　　•　　　•　　　•　　　•

Mark opened his paper to the Local News section. He read the headline: "BIG WINNER AT DIRTY SAM'S." Greta Robinson was pictured with her arm around—could it be?—Herb Pine. He read the story. "Ten grand. That guy has some lucky streak."

Ted walked in and sat. "Ted, our friend Mr. Pine is in the news again."

"Oh, so you heard. He just has a graze wound. Forensics is checking the bullet now."

Mark put down the paper. "Okay, I missed something. The paper says he won ten thousand on the slots. How was he wounded?"

"He was shot in the parking garage shortly after."

"Someone after the money?"

"I don't think so. A shot from behind, then the shooter disappeared."

An officer stood in the doorway, waiting for Mark to wave him in. He handed a folder to Ted, who opened it and examined a photo. "We'll I'll be. The bullet has the same caliber and markings as the one that killed Vincent Ferrante, nine millimeter." He handed the photo to Mark. "Somebody's out there shooting up Dirty Sam's."

•　　　•　　　•　　　•　　　•

Evers Wilson read the story of Herb's lucky spin. "That guy leads a charmed life," he muttered.

"Who's that, Dad? You can't mean Herb Pine?"

He turned. "LaVonne. You're early for lunch. Can you believe this? Pine won ten thousand on a slot."

She leaned over his shoulder and read the story. "Is there anything about someone shooting at him?" She stood and sighed. "He just missed being shot on his cycle in the parking garage. Same way as Vincent Ferrante, back-to-front, shattered his windshield. Lucky for him, he saw the gun and ducked."

Evers leafed through the paper. "Nothing here. How do you know that?"

She turned to her father. "I came upon the scene, apparently a few moments after the shot. Herb was sitting still like Vincent. But he was alive."

Evers dialed Mark. "Come over here, Mark," he said into the phone. "We have to figure out what's going on. Nobody's shooting up my town. This isn't Dodge for Christ's sake."

•   •   •   •   •

Mark and Ted walked into the reception area of the mayor's office. Susie, his receptionist, was eating an egg salad sandwich and reading the horoscopes. "I see two handsome men coming into your life," Mark said.

Susie looked up. "Chief Porfino and Detective Hanson. This must be my lucky day." She flipped the page to the front of the local news. "Not as lucky as this Pine guy, though. First, he wins ten thousand dollars on the slots, then, I hear from Evers, he ducks before a bullet ruins his 'fro."

The men laughed. "Never thought of it as an afro," Mark said. "Anyway, we're here to see Evers about just that."

Susie pressed the intercom. "Mark and Ted are here, Mayor."

"Ok," Evers responded.

"Go in; he ordered lunch. Should be here in a few minutes."

They entered and saw LaVonne seated in a guest chair, twirling her hair. Evers was tapping into his smartphone. "Have a seat, gentlemen. Lunch will be here in a minute. Do either of you play Candy Crush Saga?" He put his phone down. "This current level is driving me crazy."

A hostess walked in and laid a tray of sandwiches, salads, bottles of water, juice, soda, bags of chips, and a dish containing brownies, chocolate chip cookies, and ring-dings. "Lunch is served, gentlemen," Evers said. "An army travels on its stomach."

Mark ripped into a ham and cheese sandwich and guzzled a Dr. Pepper as Ted played with a salad. LaVonne worked through a chicken salad on a poppy seed bagel, while Evers dismantled an Italian hoagie. "So, how's it going with the shootings at Dirty Sam's?" Evers asked. "How can we have two such events within a few days? This isn't a war zone."

Ted put down his fork. He started to talk, then stopped when he remembered that LaVonne was there. "You can talk in front of LaVonne. I doubt if she plugged both men," Evers said.

"It looks like the same shooter. The bullets are the same, nine millimeter. Vincent and Herb Pine knew each other. We just haven't made a connection yet."

Evers walked to the window, his napkin dangling from his open collar. "What do you think of this Pine guy? Seems pretty creepy to me."

Mark wiped his hands in a napkin. "I checked him out. No priors. He doesn't have a listed home address, just a P.O. box in Forked River."

Evers waved to someone outside, smiled, removed his napkin, and sat. "That Mrs. Galley. What a character. She was drinking a soda and looking up at my office. I wonder what she does when she's not working. Seems like she's everywhere."

He unwrapped a Ring Ding, dipped it into his Coke, and took a bite. "Mmmmppphh, mmmmpphh, mmmmpphh," he said. He saw the confusion in his visitors, wiped his mouth, guzzled his soda, and cleared his throat. "What's your plan, gentlemen?"

"We go where the evidence leads us, Mayor," Mark said. "Ted and I discussed this. He's going to Forked River tomorrow to check on Pine, watch his P.O. Box, and ask around. Someone must know him. You can't hide a seven foot frame, especially if you're covered with hair." Mark stood and walked to the window. Mrs. Galley waved. "I'm going to talk to Mrs. Galley. I saw her at the casino talking to Carla yesterday." He looked at Evers. "You're right. I wonder if she fits into all this."

•　　　•　　　•　　　•　　　•

(Friday the 17th)
Ted left Route 9 and drove toward Forked River. He stopped at a Wawa and drank a 24-ounce coffee while he checked his map for the post office. He navigated the winding streets until he saw a USPS trucks parked in a small lot. He found a space, put on his suitcoat, and pulled his badge. A few strides toward the door were enough to energize the bold Wawa Colombian. Ted spun around seeking any restaurant or facility offering relief. He knew he didn't have time for enquiries, so he hurried into the lobby and flashed his badge to a uniformed man behind the counter. "Police business. Where's your men's room."

The clerk led him to a small powder room. "Is there a problem, Officer? Should we clear the building?"

"I'll let you know in a few minutes." He rushed into the privy and dropped his trousers just in time.

He left, sighed, and returned to the lobby. The clerk was talking to what appeared to be a supervisor, while pointing at Ted. The man walked over. "Detective, I'm John Taylor, post office manager. Is there a problem?"

"There was, John. I'm okay now." He pulled his notebook. "I'm looking for P.O. Box 279, and the person who rents it."

John led Ted to the bank of boxes. "There's 279, Detective. I'd like to help you, but I'm afraid you need a subpoena to get a name." He leaned forward. "I can tell you that the mail is retrieved around noon." He glanced at the clock on the wall. "That's twenty minutes from now. "Grab a slice at Louie's pizza across the street and come back."

Ted walked into Louie's, ordered a plain slice with a diet coke, and sat. A woman walked in, head to toe hair. The cook slid a Sicilian into the oven, turned and smiled. "Shirley. Nice to see you." He looked around. "Where's your man, Herb?"

• • • • •

Ted sat in silence as Shirley downed two slices of pepperoni while inhaling a 32-oz. Mountain Dew. She stood, collected her paper plate and cup, shoved them into an already full trash can, wiped her hands together, walked to Ted, and sat. "So, young man. Why the interest in me? The hair covering my body? If you must know it's called hirsutism. Excessive body hair on a woman. My friends are ok with it and so am I." She tilted her head. "Or maybe you just get turned on watching a full-bodied female wolf down food."

Ted played with his paper cup. "No, ma'am. I was wondering how such an incredible female is single. I don't see a ring."

She smiled. "If you must know, I have a steady boyfriend. He's easily a foot taller than you and could pound you into the ground if I asked him to."

"Lucky guy. I'm from Long Harbor. Just passing through."

She smiled. "A bit ironic, I'd say. My boyfriend is in Long Harbor now. He's in the casino gaming business."

"Ah, Dirty Sam's."

"That's right."

"He's probably cleaning out the place right now," said the cook. Shirley gave the man a death stare. He looked down to break the trance, sprinkled mozzarella on a pie, slid a paddle under the work-in-progress, and shoved it into the oven. He walked to the back, eyes lowered.

"You know, you're pretty dressed up for this part of town." She sat back. "I bet you're a cop, or maybe a private dick."

"Ted Hanson, lead detective for the Long Harbor Police." He reached for his badge.

"No need for the metal, detective, I believe you." She smiled. "And I bet you even know my boyfriend, Herb Pine."

• • • • •

Ted ordered another slice as Shirley left Louie's and walked to the post office. A few minutes later, she came out with a handful of mail, kick started a Harley, and sped out of the lot. Ted dumped his plate and cup, and turned to the cook. "You see Shirley and her boyfriend often?"

"Now and then. Nice people, generally, but they can turn on you in a second." He flipped a pie. "I wouldn't mess with them if you don't have to. They're not normal. I've seen squirrels run up a tree when they're near. Saw a cat do the same thing. They know something we don't know."

"Do they live in town?"

"Out in the woods is what I hear. Off of Route 9. He claims he's a hunter and trapper, but I think he's after larger game. Hits the casinos regularly, and, I hear, almost always wins."

The cook opened the oven, removed a pizza, and guided it into a box. He sliced the pie into eight pieces, closed the box, and wrote "#18 PM" on the side. "Pepperoni and Mushroom, Officer. A favorite." He laughed. "Herb and Shirley keep asking for squirrel and raccoon. Their little joke." He opened the oven again, slid the paddle under a white pizza, and rotated it. "At least I hope they're joking."

CHAPTER 5

Mark crossed the busy street, stopping short as a young driver ran through a yellow light turning red. "Mother—" he started to say when he saw an elderly woman standing on the opposite sidewalk starting to cross. He tipped his hat as she approached.

"Mother fucker, Chief," she said. "Why are these damn kids in such a hurry these days? For two cents, I'd kick that kid right in the nuts."

He laughed. "You're right, ma'am. Nobody teaches manners these days."

The light turned green. Honking ensued as they stood in the intersection. Mark pulled his badge, gestured cars in both directions to stop, and then guided the woman across the street. He turned, held up his badge again, and crossed before anyone could object to the delay to their lives.

He opened the door to Harbor Florists. Cowbells chimed. He waited until the lone customer left, then approached the counter.

"Chief Porfino. I saw you with Mrs. McGinley in the intersection. You must be a good influence. She didn't flick anyone the bird."

Mark laughed. "I guess people know not to mess with our senior citizens."

Mrs. Galley sorted orchids. "Prom season, Chief. It's one of our busiest times." She wiped her hands on her apron. "So, what brings you over today? Buying flowers for your lovely wife?"

"I guess it wouldn't hurt. I'll take a mixed bouquet."

Mrs. Galley walked to the refrigerator, selected a colorful arrangement, added some baby's breath, wrapped it in floral paper, and then placed them in front of Mark. "Fifteen dollars, Chief. Sure to impress the wife."

Mark paid and sniffed the flowers. "So, Mrs. Galley. I saw you in Dirty Sam's the other day. You were talking to Carla Ciccone. I guess it's a small world."

"We were discussing the death of my nephew, Vincent Ferrante. The poor man was shot in his car." She pulled out a Kleenex, blew, and examined the tissue as if the boogers would reveal the killer. She shrugged and tossed it in the trash.

"I saw you too, Chief. You were talking to a tall, dark man, Herb Pine, a regular in Dirty Sam's." She smiled. "I hear someone took a shot at him too, yesterday. What's happening to our small town?"

"I'm trying to figure that out, myself. For the moment, I'm helping Detective Hanson look into Vincent's death. I didn't know he was your nephew. Maybe we can discuss him later when you're not so busy. Can we talk after you finish for the day?"

"I'd be thrilled, Chief. Come over to my house around five. One-thirteen Maple. I'll make espresso."

•   •   •   •   •

Mark rang the doorbell. "Coming, Chief," he heard along with feet shuffling and a cat squealing. The front door opened. "One moment," Mrs. Galley said. She opened the screen door and a calico hurried out. "Ms. Spots. My live-in companion. Come in."

He wiped his feet on the mat and walked into a large foyer. A small writing desk held unopened mail and a manila envelope underneath the blotter. Leona motioned Mark to the next room. "Please have a seat while I pour the espresso."

Mark sat on the couch and studied the room. A print of a seaside landscape dominated one wall. On the wall opposite, a cabinet held a long, black, metallic object. *Is that some kind of weapon? Looks like a hunting scope.* He stood and walked over to examine it. *A crossbow!* He leaned in closer.

"That's a Ravin R15," Leona said, causing Mark to jump. "It can split an apple on your head from 100 feet."

He turned to see Leona holding a tray. "Do you hunt, Mrs. Galley?"

"Please call me Leona, Mark...if I can call you Mark." She put down the tray and positioned cups of steaming liquid. She then set out two plates, and opened a box of Lorna Doones.

"Mark is fine, Leona. Do you hunt?"

"It's my passion, Mark. There's no better feeling that seeing prey at the end of an arrow. It lets Mother Nature know who's boss."

She smiled. "I know. Florist by day, and a hunter at night and weekends. Pretty odd, yet both interests say the same thing, don't they? Humans have dominion over the land. Woe to the meek. They may inherit the Earth, but the strong have first pickings."

Mark walked back to the couch, sat, and picked up his espresso. He took a sip and gasped.

"Sorry. It's served steaming hot, Mark," she said. "Have a few Lorna Doones. They provide a contrast, and soothe the tongue."

He bit into a cookie, felt instant relief, and nodded. "I'll let it cool."

Leona lifted her cup, downed half the fluid, and set it down. "Aaaahhhh, that's good. Nothing like fresh espresso." She dabbed her mouth. "Now, Mark, what do you want to ask me?"

He took out his notebook. "I didn't know you were Vincent Ferrante's aunt."

"Yes. He was my sister's boy. Pretty rambunctious as a child. I'm afraid he fell in with bad elements as an adult."

"Mario Gallante?"

"A small time hood, if you ask me. Numbers, football betting, anything to make a buck. Vincent got a job with him, and, honestly, was Mario's muscle. Not someone an aunt brags about."

She popped a cookie into her mouth, sucked the life out of it, and finished the rest of her cup. "He told me he was done with Mario. Was going to branch out by himself. He said he had something big planned. Didn't say what." She smiled. "He also met a nice girl, who he was going to introduce to me." She frowned. "Until some coward shot him."

●　　　●　　　●　　　●　　　●

Mark thanked Leona for the espresso and her time. He stood, walked into the foyer, and glanced at the manila envelope.

"I forgot to ask, Chief. Did Linda like the flowers you bought?"

"They're still in the car. I'm sure she'll like them. You have good taste."

"I have this pretty vase in the cellar. Let me get it."

Leona hurried into the kitchen. A door squeaked and Mark heard footsteps descending. "Now, where is that vase?" he heard.

He lifted the blotter and removed the envelope. "Oh, here it is. I'll just wash it off quickly, Chief, and you can have it." A faucet turned on.

Mark opened the envelope. 'IT'S HIM' was written on a sticky note. A photo. He pulled it out. *Well, well. Herb Pine.*

He heard footsteps ascending and slid the picture back into the envelope. He reapplied the sticky note and placed it back under the blotter. He stepped away from the desk and pretended to admire the framed print on the wall.

"Here it is, Chief. It will bring out the colors in your flowers."

"Thanks, Leona. Linda will love this, I'm sure."

He opened the door, and had to juggle the vase as the cat ran back in. He nodded. "Thanks again."

"Come any time, Mark. Say hello to your lovely wife."

Mark smiled and walked to his car, waving one last goodbye. As he backed into the street he wondered what 'IT'S HIM' meant.

•　　　•　　　•　　　•　　　•

Herb parked his Harley, with a new windshield, in the clearing, pulled out a box of candy from the saddlebag, and walked toward a domed grassy hut. "Yoo hoo, Lucy, I'm home."

Light emerged from the front. Shirley walked out and stood before her man. "Very funny, Herb." She spotted the Asher's. "Those better be buttercreams. No jelly filled like last time."

Herb pursed his lips and leaned forward. "Give me some sugar, my little nonpareil."

Shirley took the box, placed it on a boulder, and hugged Herb so hard, she bent him back. Hair-covered faces met and emitted groans and sucking sounds loud enough to scurry nearby wildlife. Shirley came up for air as Herb fell back, supporting himself on a tree trunk. She grabbed the box of candy. "Now let's get inside and finish what we started."

Herb stood and followed Shirley. "Oh, by the way, I met one of your friends today, Herb. Ted Hanson of the Long Harbor Police. Small world, huh?" She dimmed the light. "He was in Louie's getting a slice and watching me. I picked up our mail. The clerk told me the detective was asking about our P.O. Box and who owned it. Why the sudden interest?"

•　　　•　　　•　　　•　　　•

Shirley rolled away from Herb. "Well, that's a surprise. Not feeling up to it today, Herb?" The big man rolled onto his back.

"I got things on my mind, Shirley," he said. "Do you remember Leona Galley?"

"The Red Dahlia?" She shivered. "Holy shit, Herb. You skipped out on her with a lot of money. Did you see her?"

Herb stood, put on pants, pushed Shirley's cat off a chair, and sat. "Yeah. She's living in Long Harbor now. She owns a flower shop, for Pete's sake. Innocent spinster by day, ruthless, violent killer when she's off the clock." He saw a deck of cards lying next to the lamp and shuffled them. "We met up at Dirty Sam's. Told me she was glad to see me and wanted the fifty grand back in one week. Plus interest and penalties. So one hundred thousand."

"Are we packing up and leaving?"

"She'll find me wherever I go. I need to come up with the money to get her off me once and for all."

"What will you do?"

"I can't rob a bank. Gotta find a place that has lots of money, easy to grab." He scratched what had to be a chin under all that fur. "Dirty Sam's, maybe. They must rake in that much each day."

"They have heavy security, Herb. You just can't say 'stick 'em up.'"

He put down the cards. "No, I guess not. I need someone on the inside." He smiled. "Looks like Vincent Ferrante was thinking the same thing. I wonder who his inside man was."

"Or inside woman, Herb. He was a pretty handsome guy. Maybe he charmed someone into helping him?"

"Hmm. Or I'm just pissing into the wind here." He reached for his shirt. "I think I'll check around anyway."

•   •   •   •   •

Ted walked past Mark's office carrying a brown, greasy bag. Mark sniffed and turned from the keyboard. "Ted, is that a mushroom cheesesteak I smell? Where's that from?"

The detective walked in and placed the bag in front of Mark. "Louie's Pizza in Forked River, Chief. I had a few slices waiting for someone to show up at Herb's P.O. Box. The cheesesteak smelled so good, I ordered one to take home. It's still warm somehow. Want part?"

Mark hurried to his office door, closed and locked it, then opened his file cabinet. He pulled a dozen paper plates, a bag of napkins, plastic forks, a bottle of catsup, and a handful of salt packets. He dumped them on the table and signaled Ted to unveil the masterpiece.

Ted removed the aluminum foil. Steam rose. "Oh my God. And it's got fried onions," Mark said. He smiled at his detective. "Ted, marry me."

"You're spoken for, Chief. Besides, I'm just another grilled beef and provolone passing through your life." He grinned. "You'll dump me for the next meatball parm who smiles at you."

Mark nodded. He swiveled and opened a small refrigerator. He removed a 2-liter Dr. Pepper. "I also have a Diet if you want, Ted."

His detective shrugged. "The real stuff is good, Mark. In for a penny, in for a pound." He broke the masterpiece in half, placing each on a paper plate. "Bon appetite."

Both men maintained a respectful silence as they stuffed meat, cheese, onions, and torpedo roll into their mouths. After a few bites, Mark sat back, reached for half a dozen napkins, wiped his mouth, chin, and shirt collar to remove wayward grease, and sighed. "This is damn good, Ted. Louie's in Forked River, you say. I'll have to make a special run sometime soon."

Ted dabbed his mouth with one napkin. He sipped the Dr. Pepper. "I ran into Herb's girlfriend there. She stopped in before going to the post office. I think she's even hairier than Herb." He smiled. "Yet, she has this sexual magnetism to her. I wonder who's on top when she and Herb fuck."

Mark gagged, coughed, and spit Dr. Pepper. "Ted, I didn't expect that from you. Not that I wasn't wondering the same thing." He sat back. "So who do you think is the brains of the pair?"

"Hard to say, Mark. I think if they paired together, they'd be pretty hard to defeat. I can't imagine anyone who could scare them off."

CHAPTER 6

Greta Robinson checked herself in the rearview mirror. *Night manager of Dirty Sam's, yet only making 60 grand a year. Well that's gonna change soon.*

She turned into the third floor parking level. Opening her purse, she pushed past the gun she used for protection, found her Mentos, popped two into her mouth, chewed, and contemplated her future. *Another couple days and I make my move. Then sayonara Dirty Sam's and Long Harbor. It's off to warmer climes, cabana boys, and bottomless margaritas.*

She swallowed the candies, rolled off two more, and leaned forward as a Brinks truck positioned itself in a lined-off area. Two men got out and entered through a non-descript orange door. A man emerged from the back of the truck and stood motionless. He saw Greta in her car, relaxed, and waved. Greta lowered her window. "Hi, Lenny. How's the wife?"

"Doing better, Miss Robinson. Should be over that nasty cold pretty soon."

After a few minutes, Charlie Klein, an assistant manager, emerged from a door with the two guards wheeling a dolly with bags of money. Lenny drew his gun and opened the back of the truck. The men placed the bags inside, then Lenny climbed in as the two men secured the door. The men nodded to Charlie, who returned to the casino, walked to the front of the Brinks and climbed in. The truck backed up, then pulled away.

"Two minutes, thirty seconds, twice a day, five p.m., and midnight," she whispered. "Once I find my new partner, we'll time this together. Then we make our move."

She pulled into a parking spot and lit a cigarette. *Fifteen minutes till my shift. I'll wait here and think this out, then pull into my reserved spot where my people will see me.*

●　　　●　　　●　　　●　　　●

Herb roared into the Dirty Sam's garage, navigated to the level where he was ambushed, and found a space near the exact parking spot. He walked over and stood at the front of the car currently occupying that space. He crouched and focused on the view behind. An unmarked door stood off at an angle. "Hmmm."

He started to walk over when the door opened, and a hostess came out, lit a cigarette, and leaned against the wall. Herb stopped. "Mr. Pine, how are you?" she called out when she noticed him. She waved her smoke. "Nasty habit I got."

Herb continued toward her. "It's Jill, right?" She nodded. "I never noticed that door before."

"It's a security door. But they don't always alarm it. It's good for getting away from the crowd and grabbing a few minutes of peace and quiet."

Herb pulled a pack from his shirt pocket. "Can I join you?"

"Sure. 'Smoke 'em if you got 'em,' my dad used to say."

He lit his cigarette. He pointed the tip toward the parking spot. *The shooter must have come out of this door.* "So do many of you use this door?"

"We're told to not use it. Management wants us close to the action and not wandering off. Plus customers frown on seeing us smoking and tapping into our phones." She turned when she saw headlights as a car pulled out of a parking spot. "Crap, it's Greta, my boss." Herb waved her to a spot behind a Hummer. He walked into the lane and stomped out his cigarette. Greta stopped short and rolled the window. "Mr. Pine. I didn't see you."

"Hi Greta. Just smokin' one before I go in." He turned toward the spot where he had been shot. "I'm still a little spooked about the other night."

"I can understand. Well, have a good evening, Mr. Pine." Greta drove off.

Jill stood and waved to Herb. "Thanks, Mr. Pine. I owe you one."

●　　　●　　　●　　　●　　　●

Greta stopped as a car with two seniors slowly pulled out of a space. *Should I really go on with this robbery? I have a decent job here, though not much of a paycheck. They'll suspect some inside job, then they'll question me. I just can't skip town. The only way this works is if I partner with someone who won't choke under pressure, won't give up anyone if questioned, and is so amoral that knocking off a casino just seems like a day's work.*

She adjusted her rearview and saw Herb walking toward the casino elevators. *Pine! Well why not? He apparently can dodge a bullet, maybe he can pull off a heist. Might as well make him a partner. Ugh. A bit hairy for my taste. Yet, sexy in some earthy way. I'll need to get closer to him. Maybe even flirt. Who knows? Maybe once you go black fur, you never go back.*

●　　　●　　　●　　　●　　　●

Herb walked to the Starbucks counter, ordered a Carmel Macchiato, left a big tip for his favorite barista, Marcy, and found a seat facing the gaming area. He took a sip of the hot drink and considered his options. A giggle from the counter. Marcy pointed to her lip.

Herb dabbed his mouth with a napkin. Whipped cream. He nodded and smiled. "Thanks," he called out. "You need a facemask to drink one of these." Marcy smiled showing perfect white teeth. *Hmmm. Too young. Plus Shirley would kill me. She might understand a prostitute as a way of blowing off steam, but not some kid working her way through college.*

Now, back to my dilemma, a hundred grand to Leona in less than a week. Herb finished his drink and started to walk to the blackjack tables. He noticed two men in white shirts, black pants, and somber expressions enter the cashier's office, each man calmly noting those standing in the vicinity. *Yep. Heavy security, but quick cash. Wham, bam, thank you, ma'am. That's my get out of jail free card from Leona. I just need to find someone on the inside with enough knowledge to let me pull this off.*

He saw Greta on her way to the cashier's. She turned to him, smiled, and seemed to wiggle, just a bit. *Is she flirting with me? She seems so serious all the time.* He smiled back and continued toward a table.

Greta stopped, turned around, and walked up to him. "Mr. Pine, good luck today. If there's anything you need from me, anything, don't be afraid to ask." She smiled. "I get off at eight. Maybe we can meet for dinner. Somewhere dark and cozy."

"I'd like that Greta. This place can be impersonal at times." He smiled. "It would be good to get to know you better."

●　　　●　　　●　　　●　　　●

Herb read the menu as Greta drank her wine. "What are you in the mood for Greta? Fish, fowl, red meat?"

She put down her glass and ran her finger over the rim. "I'm into anything, Herb. I have a voracious appetite."

Herb tried to regain focus as Greta's stockinged foot ran up and down his pant leg. "I'm partial to wild game, myself."

"They have venison," Herb said.

"Anything I can put in my mouth and suck the life out of, Herb," she replied.

Herb gagged on his Bud, then dabbed his mouth with a napkin. "Wrong pipe."

Greta smiled. "So Herb. I hear they call you the Devil." She slathered a dinner roll with butter and took a healthy bite. "How'd you get that nickname? Have you been a bad boy?"

Herb laughed. "You know how names just seem to stick? I've been hunting and trapping in the Pines all of my life." He waved his hands. "And I carry around enough hair to remind my friends of the Jersey Devil." He smiled. "I ask you, do you think I'm a wild animal?"

"We'll find out, Herb. We'll find out."

•   •   •   •   •

An hour later, Herb rolled off Greta, caught his breath, and stared at the ceiling. "That was amazing. Where did you learn that?"

"Something I learned in the convent," she laughed. "It gets cold and lonely there, so, as they say, practice makes perfect." Herb stood, walked to the bathroom, and closed the door. Fluid hitting porcelain disturbed the quiet. After 30 seconds, the sound stopped. Herb started whistling "Born to Be Wild" as the sound resumed. Another half minute. *He's a damn Gargoyle.*

Herb returned and reached for the remote control. "The only thing better than this would be if the Sixers were on." He searched, averaging about two seconds per channel. "No game tonight, damn."

Greta rose, wrapping the sheet around her. She flipped the light in the bathroom and sat on the heated toilet. Herb pressed mute and listened. *That's the sexiest tickle I've ever heard.*

She returned and pulled the remote from his hand. "How about this?" She entered "01," sat on the edge of the bed, and pointed to the screen. "The hotel channel." The voice-over explained the amenities at Dirty Sam's. The camera took a panorama of the gaming area. "We pull in a half a mil a day from gambling and entertainment," Greta said. "Most of that is cash. Two hundred and fifty grand each pickup."

"How often is that?"

Twice a day," she said, pulling the sheet over her hardened nipples. "One of my tasks is to make sure the guards are met at the security door. They're prompt and efficient. They come in, walk to the cashier's, cart the money back to the Brink's van, and drive away. It all takes about three minutes."

Herb removed her sheet, and guided her back to the bed. He slid on top. "You've got me excited. When do you have to get back to work?"

"Thirty minutes," she said. "Can you pull this off?" She smiled. "Round two, I mean. The next pickup is in an hour. Wouldn't pay for me to be humping a guest while the money is being transported."

"I stand at the ready, Miss Robinson. Wouldn't want to impede the night manager on her appointed rounds."

Greta reached beneath the blanket, found Herb's penis and smiled. "It does seem that you're ready. Let's talk later about how easy it would be to divert that money." She smiled. "That is, if you're interested in such matters."

Herb smiled. "I am. Man does not live by nookie alone."

"You sweet talker. Now let's get this deal moving."

•   •   •   •   •

LaVonne continued her rounds. As she passed each row of cars, she moved her flashlight in a wide arc. *A quiet night, so far. No gunfire, no shooting victims, just a low key shift at Dirty Sam's.* She recognized an elderly woman, blue hair swirled in a Marge Simpson beehive, as she left the parking elevator. She smiled at LaVonne and gave a thumbs up. "Had a good day, LaVonne. Hit big on the slots. Now to Birds of a Feather. It's male entertainer night. Need to see some dicks bulging from skimpy underwear."

LaVonne stifled a laugh. "Miss Lynch, I marvel at your energy." She waved a finger. "Be gentle with those young men. They don't know what they're getting into."

"With any luck, they'll be getting into me. A woman does not live by bonus spins alone."

LaVonne giggled. "Be careful out there."

Headlights approached. "Ah, the Brinks truck," said Miss Lynch. "I'll leave you to your duties." She laughed. "And I can't leave my boys waiting. They've come to depend on me."

LaVonne walked next to an SUV and watched as the truck pulled up to the security door. One of the men spoke into a cell phone as he opened the passenger side door and jumped out, joined by another guard who left by the driver side door. A third guard left by the rear and stood sentry.

The security door opened. Greta Robinson held it as the men wheeled a cart past her. She held the door for a few more seconds, then smiled, nodded, and closed the door.

LaVonne looked around. *I wonder who she nodded to.*

●　　　●　　　●　　　●　　　●

(Saturday the 18th)
Leona pulled into the IHOP across from the Day's Inn. She asked for a window booth and ordered pancakes.

At 10:30 sharp, Mario left his room, shielded his eyes from the late morning sky, and spotted the restaurant in the distance. He jumped into his Hummer and drove the hundred yards, parking in a handicap spot by the front door. He pulled a placard from his briefcase, and placed it prominently on his dashboard.

Leona shook her head. *That fat bastard. Pretending to be disabled just to get a good spot.* She left a good tip, nodded to the waitress, and walked out. She opened her glove compartment, removed a knife, took a flower from a bouquet on the passenger seat, and walked to the side of the Hummer out of Mario's view. Pulling the knife, she punctured the rear tire enough to cause a leak. She took the red dahlia and slid it into the door jam.

Mario finished his meat lover's omelet, emptied his coffee cup, and paid his bill. He bought a newspaper and left, whistling as he approached his car. Something didn't seem right. He circled around the back and saw the rear tire hugging the ground. "Shit," he called out.

He dialed AAA and stood waiting. He glanced at his watch, 11:15. *I'll put the placard away, leave a note for the driver to pick me up in my room, and, dammit, walk all the way back to the Day's Inn.* He pressed the unlock button on his keychain and reached for the door handle. The flower fell from the jam. "A red dahlia," he said. "Shit." He spun around, no one suspicious. *Could it be?*

He shuffled to his room, increasing his gait as the dark roast coffee activated his bowels. "What's that on my door," he mumbled. He stopped and crapped his pants. A metal arrow had split the peep hole.

●   ●   ●   ●   ●

Leona pulled into the Pinelands, parked her car, rubbed black camouflage makeup on her face and pulled her crossbow from the trunk. She put on her hunting gear and walked deep into the woods. A squirrel dashed by. *Too small, no sport there.*

She pulled a carbon bolt from her quiver, loaded it, and waited. She saw a possum, 50 feet away, disappearing into a burrow. Leona shrugged, too small. She brushed off a stump, pulled a cloth from her backpack, placed it neatly over the moist growths peeking out, and sat.

She lit a joint, sucked away, and glanced skyward to admire the beauty of the forest canopy protecting her from the noon sun. A rustle sounded from a nearby brush. A grey fox searching for a meal. Leona stubbed her smoke and lifted the bow. She released the latch, cocked the trigger, and moved into position.

The fox stopped foraging and turned in time to see the carbon bolt pierce its skull. Leona applied the latch, placed the bow on the stump, and walked over to retrieve her prey. She lifted the arrow and admired the animal dangling in front of her. Pulling a knife, she gutted the victim, letting the internal organs and blood drip onto the ground. She pulled the bolt, struggling to work it free from the bone.

She returned to her stump, placed the carcass into a canvas carrier, and relit the joint. Minutes later, a raccoon wandered by, drawn to the scent of the blood. It nosed around for a few minutes, then fell over when the bolt pierced its chest. Leona walked over and performed the same surgery as for the fox. She placed the raccoon next to the first victim, closed the bag, and started toward her car. *This was nice. Communing with nature. Plus it keeps me in practice when I go after larger prey, like maybe that fat pig, or two-footed furry creatures.* She pulled her pocket watch. *Have to get off to my shop. Those roses aren't going to de-thorn themselves.*

•   •   •   •   •

Mark checked his email. *There's one from Mario, hmm.* He opened the message:

Mark:

Had to leave town in a hurry. Won't be back for a while. I can wire some money for Vincent's funeral expenses, but cannot attend myself.

Watch your back!
Your friend,
Mario

That's odd. Why drop his investigation, Mark wondered. *Mario doesn't back off once he gets his teeth into something. And what does "Watch your back" mean? Did something, or someone, spook him? Oh, well. Have to tell Mrs. Galley that she can arrange the funeral if she wants. Otherwise, the city will have to do it.*

Mrs. Galley. Man, there's an odd bird. I don't think she's as innocent as she looks. Better check on her history. He searched his crime database. No results. He sipped his Wawa Columbian, took a bite of a soft pretzel, and drummed his desk. He typed "crossbow" under weapons. Hundreds of hits listing them as instruments of crime. He narrowed the search to east coast states, and finally New Jersey. Still quite a few. How about "women." Less than men but still a decent number.

One entry made him sit up. No name, but an alias. *The Red Dahlia.* Very dangerous. Seems to favor a Ravin R15. He left the police database and googled crossbows and searched for the weapon. Pretty expensive. Equipped with carbon bolts, a high quality site, and other upgrades, and you were talking two or three grand. Very accurate. Not for the weekend warrior. This was a predator's weapon of choice.

Ted walked in, saw Mark engrossed, and walked behind. "Hi, Boss."

Mark jumped. "Shit, Ted. Say something next time." He pointed to the screen. "A Ravin R15. Can drop an animal or a human before they know what hit them." He turned the screen toward Ted. "Guess who owns one."

Ted shrugged.

"Sweet, little Mrs. Galley from Harbor Florists."

•　　　•　　　•　　　•　　　•

Later that afternoon, Mark walked into the flower shop and browsed as Leona waited on a customer. He nodded to the young lady as she left, then examined some potted plants as Leona pruned rose stems. Without looking up, she said, "How can I help you, Mark?"

"Mrs. Galley, Mr. Gallante had to leave town on short notice. I know he intended to arrange for Vincent's burial but looks like he's leaving that to us. Would you like to get involved?"

Leona smiled. "Hmmm, I wonder why he went away so abruptly. Seems callous." She snipped the stem off a rose. "Of course, I would be happy to do this. He was my nephew after all. When will the body be released?"

"First thing Monday, I would think. We're awaiting toxicology results. If all is clear, we can release the body."

"Ok, Mark. I'll call Danzetti's and start the process."

He seemed uncertain how to proceed.

"Is there anything else?"

He fiddled with a vase. "Linda loved the cut flowers you sold me, Leona. Our anniversary is coming up. I was looking for a gift idea. Something floral, but different."

"What does she like?

"She likes bright blooming flowers. Something she can plant."

"Mums are nice," Leona said. "And easy to care for."

Mark sniffed an African Violet. "When she was growing up, her Mom would plant Dahlias."

He checked Leona for a reaction. "I understand they're hardy."

She smiled. "That's a good choice, Mark. I'm partial to them myself. Any particular color catch her eye?"

"Red," he said, picking up a Portulaca.

Leona nodded toward the flowering plant. "Now that's a fine, hardy flower you have there, Mark. I hope you don't have a dog or cat? It can be poisonous to them."

She walked over and examined the multi-colored growth. "You have to be careful what you ask for. Flowers should bring happiness without being dangerous to yourself or others."

Picking up a pink plant, she continued. "Now, this is a *Survivor Dahlia*, Mark. Not red, but a nice pink. Not the blood red ones that might remind someone of injury or misfortune."

She peeked at Mark through the flowers. "Believe me, this is a much better choice."

"I'll keep that in mind, Leona. Have to get back to work." Mark walked out, nodding to her as he closed the door.

Leona smiled, put the plant back on the table and walked to the register. "Amateur," she muttered. "And not very subtle."

•   •   •   •   •

Evers walked into Harbor Florists and waited as Leona finished with a customer. He nodded to the young man as he walked out with Peonies. Evers pulled daisies from the refrigerated display case and placed them on the counter in front of Leona. "Mayor Wilson. How are you? I seem to be entertaining Long Harbor royalty today. Chief Porfino was in here an hour ago."

"Small world, I guess," he said.

"I saw you talking to that mysterious gambler, Herb Pine, at Dirty Sam's. I guess everyone in this small town knows each other."

"I make it a point to know everyone, Mrs. Galley. I may be fairly new to town, but after years in the marines, and seeing combat, you get to feel the presence of those around you." He saw the orchids Leona was placing into gift boxes. "Ah, spring social time. Those high school kids still follow tradition. That's comforting."

Leona smiled. "I see you have Gerbera daisies, very colorful. A gift for some lucky lady?"

"For my daughter, LaVonne. I thought I'd cheer her up. She's been wandering into crime scenes lately. First, that poor Vincent Ferrante, then Mr. Pine, himself. Lucky for Pine he knows when to duck."

Leona grimaced and started to wrap the daisies. "Oh, how insensitive of me. Vincent was your nephew, I hear. Don't worry, Mrs. Galley, I have my best men on it, Chief Porfino and Detective Hanson. We'll weed out the criminal element in this town and make it safe again for folks just like you and me."

"Mayor, I appreciate that. I think my nephew was in over his head. In this world, there's the hunter and the hunted. The cops and the robbers. Sometimes, it's hard to tell them apart. She sighed. "You know that from Iraq, I guess. What's the expression? 'The enemy of my enemy is my friend?'" She taped the paper holding the daisies. "Twelve ninety-nine, Mayor. Keep them in water and they should last a week."

Evers pulled a twenty from his wallet. "I hope we can be friends, Mrs. Galley. There's too many enemies in this world."

"True enough, Mayor," she said handing him the flowers. "In the meantime, keep your hunting skills sharp. You never know when you'll need them."

CHAPTER 7

Mark opened the Krispy Kreme box and marveled at the assortment the clerk had chosen for him. "Nothing healthy here, but damn interesting." Ted shrugged and chose a chocolate crème. "Might as well go for it," Ted said.

The men studied the surveillance footage around Herb's shooting. "Did you notice this was on the same floor and the same general vicinity of Vincent's shooting?" said Ted.

"Yeah, I was thinking that also. Do you think it's a coincidence?"

"No, I think the killer knew the men's habits and took advantage of it."

Mark sat back. "So Vincent and Herb pissed off the same person. Another gambler, someone working at Dirty Sam's?"

"I would think so. Where are the vantage points for these shootings? I don't think they were drive-bys"

Mark closed the screen. "Ok, Ted. Get someone on these angles. One: did anyone leave the vicinity after these shootings? Two: if not, where could the shots have come from?"

"Ok, Mark. Maybe I'll talk to LaVonne again. See what she thinks."

Mark spun his chair around and glanced out over the plaza, two stories below the office. "Be careful with her. Another coincidence is that she came upon both crime scenes first. Probably nothing to it, but we need to follow all of the threads."

He focused on Harbor Florists across the street. No Mrs. Galley, just a young clerk switching on the evening lights as dusk settled in. "Mrs. Galley must have left for the day, Ted. I wonder how she spends her Saturday evenings." He turned to his lead detective. "She's a real mystery, that woman. And as Vincent's aunt, I wonder if she's tied up in all these events."

"Do you think she'd kill her own nephew?"

Mark shook his head. "No, she seemed to care for Vincent. Plus, that would be a rather cold-blooded way to express disapproval." He examined the picture of the Ravin R15 he had printed from the Cabela's web site. "Plus, guns aren't her M.O. She's a crossbow person. A predator in a world of prey."

•   •   •   •   •

Ted walked into the casino, found an empty baccarat table manned by his favorite dealer, and cashed in $200. "Do you mind if we wait for a few others to join?" the dealer asked.

"No problem, Phil." He ordered a Sam Adams, and swiveled to look over the casino activity for the night. "Not many people on a Saturday," he said to the dealer.

"We get a later crowd. It's still a bit early."

Greta Robinson walked by. She smiled as the men watched her enter the cashier's office.

A dark mass entered Ted's field of vision. Herb Pine. He pulled a chair next to him, smiled at Phil, and pulled a wad of cash. "Five hundred, my man. I'm feeling pretty lucky tonight."

Phil dealt, just Jim and Herb playing. After a few minutes, Herb was up 200, and Ted down to his last 25. Ted pushed his last chip forward and awaited his cards. Phil, Herb, and Ted stopped for a minute as Greta passed. All three men smiled. Greta winked, enjoying her mastery of the situation.

After she disappeared behind a large display advertising Jeff Dunham, Ted turned to the men. "I never realized how hot she was." Herb nodded. Phil dealt. "You have no idea," Herb and Phil said at the same time.

●   ●   ●   ●   ●

Ted cashed out, having won 500. *That was nice. Now I'm only down a couple of grand for the year.* He passed a slot showing Simpsons characters. He checked the betting options. *I can do three dollars a spin.* Ten minutes later, his 500 was reduced to 150.

"Better to quit while you're ahead, Detective. You never know which direction your fortunes will take."

Ted nodded, took his credit slip, and stood. "I think, you're right, Miss Robinson. A fool and his money, I guess."

"You can call me Greta, Detective," she said, touching his shoulder. Ted swelled with something besides pride. "Can I have a hostess get you a drink?"

She rubbed his sleeve. "Or we can get one together." She smiled. "In a more intimate setting, I hope."

"I'd like that, Greta. Call me Ted." He looked around, more to quell his passion than to investigate his surroundings. "When do you get off?"

"It depends on who I'm with. Sometimes I get off multiple times."

Ted was melting quickly. He sat, or more accurately, fell into the chair of a Wild Buffalo slot and fumbled for his notebook. "Are you free at eleven?"

Greta laughed. "I am, Ted. See you at the Golden Ore lounge." She pointed to the stampeding buffalo on the screen. "Be sure you don't get run over, Ted. This is dangerous territory."

After a few minutes, enough blood returned to his brain to allow Ted to focus on his plan for the night. He took the elevator to the ground level, flashed his badge, and asked the associate at the security booth for LaVonne Wilson. The associate checked her screen. "She's doing her rounds. Should be on three according to her last check in."

Ted hurried into an elevator, sardining himself into the crowd of excited revelers. Most got off at Casino level, leaving him alone with an elderly couple who were checking the entertainment brochure. "I love that Jeff Dunham. And that Achmed the dead terrorist. He's a real hoot." The door opened for three. As Ted walked out, they shouted "I keel you."

He smiled at the couple, nodded, and walked down a long row of cars looking for LaVonne. *Man, it's pretty lonely here. Endless cars, but no people.* He saw a beam of light off to the left. *There she is.* He scooted between BMWs, Toyotas, SUVs, even a motorcycle, and walked to LaVonne. She smiled when she recognized him. "Detective, how are you. I didn't expect to see you. Playing the tables tonight?"

Ted grinned. "I did OK at Baccarat, then lost most of it on the slots."

LaVonne laughed. "Like they say, 'the house always wins.'"

Ted snorted. "That's true, I guess. I think people are just buying a few hours of escape, with the hope that they'll be the one hitting the jackpot."

"Well, I must be on my way, Detective. Have to keep things safe for the gaming public."

"Actually, I wanted to talk to you about the recent shootings," Ted said. "You were the first to discover Vincent Ferrante *and* Herb Pine."

"Just my luck, Detective. Plus, I guess, more things happen at night. People drink, maybe they lose large amounts, get into it with other gamblers." She sighed. "The day shift has it easier. Some tipsy seniors, rowdy folks on tour busses. Easy to handle. And no one takes a shot at anyone."

She pointed toward the elevators. "There's the hot spot, Detective. Both shootings on this level, both in the same area."

"So do you have a theory on this, Miss Wilson?"

"Well, I'm no detective. But what do you say: motive and opportunity? Not sure of any motive, except both men seemed to attract attention. Maybe they knew something or did something that makes them dangerous to have around. I have no doubt that the shootings are connected."

She nodded to the security door. "In terms of opportunity, that orange door over there is a nice vantage point. A quick shot, close the door and on your way."

"So you think an employee is involved."

"Maybe. Some high rollers also get access to the door. A quick escape route where they don't have to mingle with the hoi polloi."

The door opened. Herb Pine walked out. He walked toward Ted and LaVonne, nodded, walked to the motorcycle, kick started it, and pulled away.

"What a character. Knows everyone here. I wonder who he pissed off enough to get a bullet through his windshield."

"Who's your money on?" Ted asked.

LaVonne laughed. "I don't gamble." She checked her watch. "With money or with lives."

Ted nodded. "A good policy."

"You know, Detective. I did see something odd yesterday. The Brinks truck came, and Greta Robinson opened the door for them and waited for their return with the take. Nothing unusual there. As the men stored the money, Greta seemed to nod to someone in the distance. I couldn't make out who, and frankly, couldn't be certain if there was anyone there, at all."

"Hmm. Do you meet the Brinks truck when it arrives?"

"No. Casino management. They treat us like rent-a-cops. We just check the parking garage and other grounds. We don't have anything to do with the money." She checked her watch again. "Look, Detective, I gotta continue my rounds. If I see anything unusual, I'll let you know."

"Thanks, LaVonne. Always good to have someone with their ear to the ground."

•   •   •   •   •

At eleven, Ted pulled a stick of gum from his pocket, unwrapped it, and popped it in his mouth. He hurried to the elevator, selected the casino level, and checked the overhead signs when he stepped out. The Golden Ore Lounge. Straight ahead. He walked past the table gaming area, and saw the darkened bar. He entered and searched for Greta. He shuddered as he felt a tap on his shoulder.

"Sorry, Detective," Greta said. "Didn't mean to scare you. Looks like we came at the same time. I like when that happens."

Ted swallowed his gum and coughed. She patted his back. "Wrong pipe, Detective. You have to be careful what you swallow."

They found a table and ordered drinks. Ted went for a Heineken, Greta ordered a boiler maker. She dropped the shot of whiskey, glass and all, into the draft beer. "Bottoms up," she said, then emptied the glass in one draw. "Aaaahhhh," she said. "That hit the spot."

Ted looked at the empty. "Another, Greta?"

"Sure. I have a room for the night. The perks of the job."

Ted signaled the waitress. "So how did you get into this business, Greta?"

She laughed. "I was doing a nine to five at a law office. It paid well, but was boooorrrrring. Filing motions, preparing papers for spouses in divorce actions, carting boxes of legal documents into courtrooms." She wiped condensation from her recently arrived drink. "I wanted more action." She laughed. "I wanted to *be* the action."

She smiled at Ted as he nursed the Heineken. "So, Detective. What made you choose a life of crime? That is, catching criminals before they can escape justice."

"I always wanted to be a cop. Protecting the public, while, in some odd way, experiencing the thrill of the pursuit."

"You know, Ted. I heard once that people become cops for the same reason that people become criminals. They both like living on the edge of the law." She reached over and touched his hand. "Didn't you ever want to do anything illegal, maybe even nasty?"

Ted's forming erection was assisted by the vibration of his cell. "I need to get this."

A text from Rhonda: *I'm lonely.*

"Duty calls, Miss Robinson. I have to be on my way."

Greta pouted. "Aw, a shame. Maybe we can do this some other time, Ted. I can get a room anytime you want to interrogate me."

Ted imagined Aaron Rogers launching a Hail Mary. That helped. Maybe he could stand without showing a pup tent. "Like I said, duty calls. Thanks for the offer."

●   ●   ●   ●   ●

Ted knocked on the door and propped up the gas station roses he bought minutes ago. Rhonda opened the door in sweatpants and a Cambria Community College sweatshirt. "Teddy, I'm so glad you came." She glanced at the bouquet. "And you brought roses. Come in, let me find a vase."

He sat on the couch and examined her small rancher. *Hmmm, all the time we got together, I was never inside her house.* On the opposite wall, a crucifix hung. Jesus, suffering for men's sins.

"That was a gift from my dad when I made my first communion." She sighed as she put the flowers peeking out of a porcelain vase on the coffee table. "I was so innocent then." She sat next to Ted and sobbed. "What have I become?"

She buried her head in his shoulder. "I'm leaving the strip club, Teddy. I can't turn tricks or dance for lonely men anymore." She pulled a Kleenex and dabbed her eyes. "Father Jim has been advising me. This is my chance to put my old life away and save myself."

Ted brushed away the hair covering her right cheek. "Rhonda, anything I can do to help."

"Stay with me tonight, Teddy. No sex, no handcuffs. Just you and me holding each other. I need the warmth of you next to me."

He was moved. "Sure, Rhonda." He nodded at the crucifix. "Maybe I need some redemption myself."

CHAPTER 8

(Sunday the 19th)

St. Augustine's church filled for the 9:30 mass. Rhonda and Ted slid into a back pew. Rhonda knelt and made a sign of the cross. Ted followed her, his knees rubbing against the kneeler in the pew in front.

He mimicked the cross gesture and shrugged as Rhonda smiled. *What now. Hi, God. I guess you haven't seen me in a while. I'm doing fine. I hope you haven't missed me.* Rhonda sat back and Ted followed. He glanced at his fellow congregants. *I know most of these people.*

A woman pointed to Rhonda, frowned, and whispered something to her young son. Rhonda saw this, leafed through her missal, and reached for Ted's hand. Ted stuck out his tongue at the woman and boy. The woman emitted an audible harrumph and opened her Sunday bulletin.

Mark walked by with Linda. He saw Ted and tapped his wife on the shoulder. Linda smiled at Ted and Rhonda and the pair entered the pew just in front. After kneeling and praying, they sat back and turned around. "Ted, Rhonda, good to see you," Mark said. He waved his arm. "And we have a nice crowd today."

A woman in a flowery dress, face covered by a veil, passed by. She screeched to a halt. "Chief Porfino and Detective Hanson. And Linda, and, I believe, Rhonda Gillmore," said Leona. "Beautiful day isn't it?" She nodded toward the stained glass image of St. Augustine. "Saints and sinners reconciled, isn't that the line from a Christmas hymn?"

She saw the woman who had sneered at Ted and Rhonda shake her head and nudge her husband. "Hello, Mrs. Callahan. Still selling cigs to minors at the Shop-n-go?" The woman reopened her missal and mouthed a reply. Leona turned to the couples. "I wonder what Christian greeting begins with an F. Maybe she said, 'Fine day.'"

•   •   •   •   •

Sheila put down her coffee as she saw the crowd emptying out of St. Augustine's. "Get ready, ladies, it's show time," she said to her wait staff. The diner filled with hungry Christians as Midge, her hostess, helped Sheila seat families.

"Table for five, Sheila," Mark said as Ted, Rhonda, Linda, and Mrs. Galley studied the dessert case.

"Sure thing, Chief." She signaled Midge and pointed to a long window booth. They slid into both sides with Mrs. Galley sitting next to Ted and Rhonda. "Aaaahhhh," she said. "The King of Queens was right. A booth is a vacation for your ass." All present laughed. "Am I right?" A murmur of agreement.

A couple in biker helmets and clad head-to-toe in leather entered. The taller one removed his headgear. The female did the same.

Mark tapped Ted's arm. "Hey, there's Herb Pine."

"And his girlfriend, Shirley," said Ted. "Remember, Mark? I met her in Forked River."

Sheila walked the pair past the booth. Herb and Shirley did a double-take as they saw Leona. Herb regained his composure. "Chief, Detective, ladies. Enjoying a Sunday breakfast?"

Mark reached out and shook Herb's hand. He waved toward Rhonda, Linda, and Leona. "This is Herb Pine, ladies, a patron of Dirty Sam's. Herb barely escaped being shot at in the casino the other night."

Herb pointed to the streak of skin on his cheek, the only part not covered with hair. "It was literally a close shave," he laughed. He smiled at his companion. "And this is my girlfriend, Shirley."

Mark did the honors. "My wife Linda, Ted's girlfriend Rhonda, and Mrs. Galley, florist extraordinaire."

Linda nodded. Rhonda smiled at Shirley, then at Herb. Leona stood and hugged Shirley. "I'm glad to meet you. I feel like I know you already."

"Ahem." Sheila stood at a nearby table, holding menus for the bikers.

"Well, our table awaits," said Herb, seeming relieved. "Enjoy your meal."

The couple sat. "Herb, that's the Red Dahlia," Shirley whispered.

"I know. We have three days to get her off our back. That's why we're in town today. To meet up with our partner and work out the details."

•   •   •   •   •

Herb and Shirley drove to the Meadows section of town—nice, single family homes, nothing fancy, but functional. They parked a block from 47 Sycamore Lane, dismounted, tied their bikes to a tree, and walked toward Greta's house.

An elderly woman pulling a child in a wagon stopped, stared, and pulled her cell. Herb walked over. "Hi ma'am. What a delightful child." He crouched. "Do you believe in wolves little boy?"

"I ain't afraid of nothin', mister."

"Glad to hear it, son." He signaled Shirley over. "Ma'am," he said addressing the obvious grandmother. "We're friends of one of your neighbors. Excuse our appearance. It was such a nice day, we had to take our cycles. I hope we didn't cause any concern."

He leaned to the boy. "Did you know you had a coin in your ear?" He reached behind the boys left lobe and pulled a Kennedy dollar. "Must belong to you."

"Gosh." He peered up at the woman. "Can I keep it, Grandma?"

"I don't know..."

Shirley pulled a fifty-dollar bill. "And this is for Grandma."

The woman smiled. "Have a nice day, you two."

•　　　•　　　•　　　•　　　•

Greta was expecting only Herb. She answered the door in open blouse, and tight shorts. Rev. Al Green played in the background. "Oh, hi, Herb." She studied her unexpected guest. "I don't believe we've met."

Shirley smiled, exposing her incisors. "I'm Shirley. Herb's girlfriend. Can we come in?"

Greta led them in and offered Sam Adams and whiskey. "Boilermakers all around?"

The couple smiled and nodded. Greta poured.

"Greta, let's put you at ease. I know you're fucking Herb. My man here isn't a one creature, er, woman man. I know that."

Herb seemed to redden if that was possible. "One of my failings, I guess."

Greta smiled, somewhat relieved. "So let's discuss our mutual interests. Relieving Dirty Sam's of a day's worth of cash."

Herb sat forward. "We need to do this by Wednesday, Thursday at the latest. I have a debt to pay and an unforgiving creditor."

"Well then, let's get down to the details." She downed her drink. "Let me get us more brain food."

Hours later, Greta woke up in bed, Shirley's arm wrapped around her, stroking her breast. Herb sat in the chair opposite the bed. "Well, you two got along just fine. I had to wedge myself between you once in a while just to get some attention."

Shirley yawned. "I like your plan, Greta. What of it I can remember."

CHAPTER 9

(Monday the 20th)

Mike Danzetti put down the coffee roll, wiped his hands on a paper napkin, and answered the phone. "Danzetti's. We look forward to serving you in your time of need."

"Hi, Mike. This is Leona Galley from Harbor Florists. I'm calling for myself. My nephew Vincent Ferrante died last week and the police released his body to my care. I want to arrange for his funeral."

"So sorry to hear, Mrs. Galley. I'll call over and arrange pickup." He checked his calendar. "When do you want the services?"

"Tomorrow. He's been dead for a week. No use in having him lie around any longer. Let's do a quick viewing and then the funeral. Can you arrange with St. Augustine's and Holy Innocents?"

"Well, it is short notice."

"Grease a few palms, Mike. The church engine runs on cash."

"I think we can arrange it. I'll make the calls."

"Good. Vincent wasn't particularly holy, but family does what family does."

"And you're arranging the flowers?"

"Yes, they'll be over this afternoon. Lilies, carnations, and red dahlias."

•   •   •   •   •

Mike called the coroner. "Dr. Fuller, Mike Danzetti here. I'm authorized by Mrs. Galley to pick up Vincent Ferrante. Can I send my men over now?"

"Sounds OK to me, Mike. I'll let Chief Porfino know. He'll call you back."

Minutes later the phone warbled. "Hi, Mike. Chief Porfino. When are you burying Vincent?"

"Mrs. Galley wants it tomorrow. I think she just wants it over with."

"Um. Look, this is a high profile case. Lots of attention. I'm going to have some plainclothesmen there. They'll blend in."

"Ok, Chief. Will you be providing security?"

"No. Don't want to overdo it or spook anyone."

•   •   •   •   •

Shirley pulled into the Dirty Sam's garage, circled until she got to the third floor and parked her Harley in a slot near a support stanchion. Approaching the casino elevator, she passed the spot where Herb was fired upon. She looked around. *Yep, there's the security door. A pretty good vantage point. Hopefully, we'll see happier times there when we relieve the guards of their burden.*

She opened the door to the atrium housing the elevators, pressed the "down" arrow and awaited the next car. She turned toward the security door. A man came out, lit a cigarette, and blew a smoke ring. He turned toward the glassed-in room, saw Shirley staring back, and waved his smoke.

The door opened. She nodded to the man and got in, standing

next to an older couple.

"There's a slots tournament today, Betty," said a man wearing an "Ask Me about My Shih Tzu" t-shirt.

Betty pulled a troll with orange hair from her purse. "I'm ready, Ike," she replied. "And Little Donald is ready, too."

The elevator descended. Shirley made eye contact with Ike. "So, tell me about your Shih Tzu."

He glanced down at his shirt and laughed. "Well, Miss, her name is Gwendolyn. Princess of Manahawkin." He took a picture from his wallet. "Just two years old. Isn't she beautiful?"

Shirley studied the picture. "She's a beauty, sir. Looks good enough to eat."

The wife gasped as Ike put the picture back into his wallet. "Never quite heard it put that way, Miss," he said, laughing. "I prefer foot-long, all-beef dogs, myself. Less hair."

The door opened. The lights of the casino cast an unnatural glow into the car. "Well, here's our stop," Shirley said. She waved a finger at the man. "Now you got me thinking of hot dogs. I'll have to wolf down a few."

Shirley started toward the food court. The couple walked straight to the slots area. She heard mumbling, then the term "odd bird" from the wife.

She found a Nathan's Famous and smiled. *Wow, this was meant to be.* Ordering three with the works, she placed her Dirty Sam's 64-ounce cup under the soda dispenser. The fluid squished into the plastic. The man she saw smoking in the garage walked by. He stopped short, turned to Shirley, and nodded.

"Eighty-one," she heard. Looking at her receipt, she walked to the counter, handed the slip to the cashier, picked up her foot longs and Dirty Sam fries, and searched for a clean table. She sat, pulled twenty or so napkins, emptied hot sauce on her first victim and took a huge bite. "Damn, that's good," she said, maybe too loud.

The counter crew laughed. Shirley saluted by hoisting her cup. She downed the 64 ounces in seconds, then let out a sigh. The crew applauded.

The man walked in, ordered a large dog and a bottled water, flashed a card, and walked toward Shirley with his tray. "Can I join you, miss?" She nodded.

"I'm Larry Harkins, the day manager here at Dirty Sam's. I haven't seen you before, but you look somehow familiar." He unscrewed the cap from his Dirty Sam's mountain water and took a sip. "I hope this isn't too forward, but would you like to meet for a drink later on?" He smiled. "I bet we have a lot in common."

•　　　•　　　•　　　•　　　•

As Shirley walked through the casino, she heard cheering from a small room off to the side. Walking over, she saw Ike and Betty pounding buttons, oblivious to the dozens of others doing the same. Once in a while, Betty would reach for Little Donald and rub the orange tuft rising from its skull. A digital timer counted down. At 00:00, a shrill alarm rang and the pounding stopped—mostly.

A man with slicked-back hair spoke into a mic. "All done, folks. Let's check the results." Betty clutched her troll while Ike stretched.

The MC announced the winners. No prize for the couple. "Balls," shouted Betty. No one seemed phased by the word choice. Everyone stood and collected cigarettes, trolls, and other lucky talismans.

Ike helped Betty with her sweater. "Maybe we'll have better luck Wednesday."

Shirley nodded to the couple as they left. "Have a great day, you two. Say hello to Princess Gwendolyn of Manahawkin for me."

As the room emptied, she saw Larry Harkins open a far door followed by two Brinks guards carrying bags. *Well, I'll be.* She checked her watch: *Five p.m. Let's see what Greta and Herb think. This could be our distraction.*

•　　　•　　　•　　　•　　　•

Larry rolled off Shirley and smiled. "Wow, that was quite a ride. Are there more like you where you come from?"

Shirley laughed. "I'm just a Jersey girl, Larry, born and raised." She brushed his cheek. "But I know what I want, and how to get it."

She rubbed his arm. "So, are you from the Garden State, Mr. Harkins? Or are you a carpet bagger, looking for easy prey?"

He smiled. "I'm from Vegas. Born in the shadow of the Strip. Casinos are in my blood."

"This casino seems like small game, Larry. Maybe a few mil in revenue a week. Nothing like a Bellagio or a Venetian."

Larry stood, walked to the window, and peeked out the shade. "No, that's true. But you have to start somewhere. The opportunity came up, I had east coast contacts, so I came here."

Shirley slid out of bed, covering herself with the sheet. "Excuse me a minute." She stepped into the bathroom and hummed a familiar tune. *Is that "Born to Be Wild?"* Larry wondered?

The toilet flushed, water ran, and she returned, without the sheet. "Are you going to stand there all day, Mr. Harkins?" she asked.

"Give me just a few minutes, Shirley. How about I open a bottle of Champaign from the mini-bar after I take care of business."

Shirley pouted, then found the remote and switched on the casino information channel. Larry returned from the bathroom, and stopped when he saw the ad showing the slots and gaming tables.

He sat next to Shirley. "You know, Dirty Sam's isn't that small. It takes in a half a mil a day. A tidy sum for a couple looking for a quick payday, and willing to take a risk. Hell, they're insured. I wonder if the Chinese owners would even lose any sleep over losing a few hundred thou."

He rubbed Shirley's thigh. "It would have to happen at night, though. Can't have the place relieved of the take during my shift. Wouldn't look good on my CV."

He realized he was ready for the next encounter. "Now, let me get that bottle, and see what we can come up with."

Shirley licked his ear. "You know, Larry. I think we can do business, you and I."

CHAPTER 10

(Tuesday the 21st)

Mark read the headline in the Long Harbor Press: *Casino Murder Victim Buried Today.* The sub headline read: *Is This the Beginning of More Violence?* Beat Reporter Lisa Channing laid out the details:

Today, Vincent Ferrante, murdered Sunday, the 12th in the Dirty Sam's parking garage, will be laid to rest in Holy Innocents cemetery after a mass of Christian Burial at St. Augustine's. A short remembrance will be conducted at Danzetti's funeral home before transport to the church. The services are expected to be well attended by city officials, close family, and the public.

This is the first murder in Long Harbor since the opening of Dirty Sam's. The licensing process for the casino was long and tumultuous with local opposition by church and civic leaders, and vocal, sometimes violent, support of trade unions and the casino industry.

Just a few days ago, a second shooting occurred in almost the same location at Dirty Sam's. In that case, Mr. Herbert Pine, resident of Forked River, and frequent patron of the casino, narrowly avoided the same fate as Mr. Ferrante, by seeing the hand of the gunman at the last moment.

What is happening to our small town? Has a criminal element moved in to claim its piece of the pie? Will Dirty Sam's become a magnet for unwelcome elements hoping to profit by terrorizing our citizenry?

What can we expect next? Mayor Wilson, Police Chief Porfino, we need answers.

"Well, what do you think, Mark? Are we seeing the beginning of some sort of shoot-em-up turf war," asked Evers. "This whole thing is giving Long Harbor a black eye."

Mark put down the paper. ""I think she's overreacting. We'll get this sorted out."

Evers walked to the window. "Let's make sure we have a presence at the funeral. Show whoever is disturbing our peace and quiet that his days are numbered."

"Or *her* days, Mayor," Mark said. "Crime is much more egalitarian these days."

Mark opened a desk drawer and pulled a pocket mirror. No ketchup on his face. Good. "We'll have men at the grave site, and a few at Danzetti's. If all goes well, maybe people will calm down."

•   •   •   •   •

Jim Cooper stepped out of his car and hurried to the passenger side to open the door for Jan. They walked toward St. Augustine's. *Boy, this doesn't get easier. I spent five years here as associate pastor and still have fond memories.* Jan took his hand.

They'd decided to skip Danzetti's, but to attend the funeral mass. Vincent was an acquaintance, but not a close friend, just brothers-in-arms at the blackjack table. They entered a pew in the back of the empty church and knelt.

Father Theo entered and nodded to the couple. Jim forced a smile. *He doesn't even know who I am. Father Ray dies and the bishop names this long haired hippy wannabe as replacement. This would have been me if I'd hung around.* Jan blessed herself and sat back. *I love Jan, though. Oh well, the choices we make.*

A long shadow interrupted his musing. He turned toward the

church entrance. The hearse stopped. Mike Danzetti hurried to the rear and waved his arm, no doubt signaling the pall bearers.

The mourners started to enter. A woman in black, veil covering her face, was first. She walked toward the front. Jan nudged Jim. "That's Mrs. Galley from Harbor Florists."

Jim followed her as she entered the first pew without genuflecting. "I think you're right. What's she doing here?" He studied those walking in. "Where's Mario?"

Carla came in next and sat next to Leona. They hugged.

Herb Pine and a hairy, but attractive, female walked in. Herb nodded to Jim who returned the gesture. Greta Robinson walked in. *Well, Dirty Sam's is represented. Makes business sense, I guess.* Greta sat behind Herb and Shirley.

Mark Porfino, Linda, Ted Hanson, and, how about that, Rhonda Gillmore walked up the aisle. The two couples sat behind Greta. Mark leaned forward and tapped her on the shoulder. They talked for a minute, with Herb joining in.

Why does this seem like a rogue's gallery instead of mourners? What do the police suspect? And where's Mario?

As if on cue, the Cambria mobster slid into the pew behind Jim and Jan. He swung his hand, possibly to make the sign of the cross, though it appeared more like preparing to rope a steer. Jim flipped open his missal and sought the funeral rite. A finger jabbed into his shoulder. Mario whispered in his ear.

"Hey, Jim, long time no see." He turned toward Jan. "And Mrs. Cooper. This brings back memories." He laughed. "But this time, you're in the peanut gallery, and not at the center of things."

Jim smiled at Mario. "Good to see you, Mario. I expected *you* to be at the center of things. Vincent was your man."

Mario's face dropped. "I was called out on business." He looked around. "A sparse crowd here. You didn't happen to see anyone who looks out of place, did you?"

"Well, Mrs. Galley from the flower shop. "Didn't expect that."

Mario mulled this over. *Mrs. Galley. I met her years ago when Silvio died. Can she be? Nah...not a chance.*

●　　　●　　　●　　　●　　　●

The funeral mass ended in a little over an hour. Jim checked his watch. *It would have been shorter if Theo didn't expound on man's inhumanity to man. Blah, blah, blah.*

Mario left his pew and hurried out the door.

Father Theo, followed by the pall bearers standing at the side of the coffin, then the attendees, walked down the aisle. Jim and Jan stood and waited for all to pass. They left the pew and walked outside. Jan and Linda, longtime friends, chatted. Mark walked over.

"Seem like old times, doesn't it, Jim?" He looked around. "I wonder if the killer is here, or keeping his or her distance."

Linda walked over with Jan. "Are you coming to the gravesite?"

Jan nodded to Jim as she took Linda's arm. "Sure. In for a penny, in for a pound," he said. They stared at Jim, confused. "I mean, we'll pay our respects."

●　　　●　　　●　　　●　　　●

Herb and Shirley started their Harleys and waited to join the line. Greta Robinson pulled behind. Jim and Jan positioned themselves behind the last car flagged with the orange funeral placard. A man from Danzetti's tapped on Jan's side window. "Put this on your dashboard," he said as he handed over one for them.

"I guess we're official now," Jim said to Jan. "At least we can run a few red lights."

They followed the procession headed for Holy Innocents Cemetery. The line of cars pulled in and wound their way to the burial site. Jan and Jim got out and stood at the edge of the mourners. Mrs. Galley glanced up and seemed to frown in Jim's direction. Jan turned around. Mario stood, head down, clearly the recipient of the stare. Jan nudged Jim. "Mrs. Galley seems to disapprove of Mario."

"This whole ceremony is unsettling," Jim responded. "Mark and Ted are studying the mourners, almost seeming to forget that someone is being buried. Herb and his girlfriend are talking to Greta Robinson, oblivious to Father Theo and Vincent, and even Mrs. Galley. She's looking at her watch, for Pete's sake."

Jim smiled. "I almost hope the coffin would open, Vincent would sit up, and say 'What the fuck, people, can't a guy get some respect here.'"

Jan laughed, maybe too loud. Father Theo stopped reciting the prayers for the dead and all focused on the couple. Jim hugged Jan, pulling her face onto his shoulder. "Sorry, grief takes all forms."

•   •   •   •   •

Herb and Shirley both placed a flower on Vincent's coffin, nodded to Carla, then to Mrs. Galley, the grieving aunt, and walked toward their Harleys. Greta dropped a carnation on the metal casket, touched it in what seemed a moment of reflection, and then spoke briefly to Mrs. Galley.

Leona smiled, nodded and responded. Greta's jaw dropped, then she regained her composure and walked off.

Mark, Ted, Linda, and Rhonda payed their respects and started to leave. Mark stopped, turned, and offered a clean handkerchief to Leona. "Thank you. Mark."

He nodded. "I hope you don't think this intrusive at this time, but what did Miss Robinson say to you."

"She said, 'We'll miss Vincent at Dirty Sam's. I hope they find the creep that shot him.'"

She tucked the handkerchief into her purse. "I told her, 'Predator and prey, Miss Robinson. The predator survives until a skilled hunter reduces it to a trophy to be stuffed and mounted.'" She watched the

Harleys leave the cemetery entrance. "I told her to be wary of friends in wolves' clothing."

•　　　•　　　•　　　•　　　•

Herb and Shirley pulled into the strip mall in front of Louie's Pizza, entered, greeting Louie himself, and ordered a large pie with pepperoni, mushroom, and green pepper.

Minutes later, Greta parked in front of the pizzeria, got out, and stretched. She leaned on her car, took a deep breath, and took in a panorama of Forked River. She turned toward Louie's and waved when she recognized the couple through the plate glass. She strode in, sniffed the aromas, smiled at the cook, and swung into the booth opposite her friends. "So what's your new angle, Shirley? I'm all ears."

"Well, as you no doubt know..." Shirley stopped when Louie himself delivered the steaming masterpiece. "It's hot, folks. Be careful." He dealt paper plates to his customers and handed napkins wrapped around a plastic fork and knife. "Enjoy."

Herb and Shirley forgot all pressing business and separated slices. They slid pieces onto their plates, making sure to catch any wayward cheese. Each blew at their plate, causing their napkins to fly across the table. Greta retrieved them and returned each to their rightful owners. Herb pointed to the pie. "Come on, Greta. Get it while it's hot."

Greta picked up a slice and lowered it onto her plate. She picked up the knife and fork, and heard a collective gasp as she attacked the pizza as if cutting into a steak. "You use a knife and fork for pizza?" Shirley questioned. "You're not from Jersey, are you?"

Greta chewed slowly, swallowed the mouthful, emitted an "ummmm," and gave a thumbs up to Louie and the cook. They beamed.

"No, I'm from a small town in Kansas. Tonganoxie, Leavenworth

County. My dad was military, an MP." She looked at her plate. "Did I commit some social crime?"

"Well, in Jersey, we eat pizza with our hands," Herb said. "But, that's ok. Dig in."

There was a tacit agreement to hold off business until the pie and enormous drinks were consumed. Herb signaled the owner. "Louie, cannolis all around." He sat back. "Now, Shirley, continue with your plan."

•   •   •   •   •

Mark and Ted returned to the station after lunching with Linda and Jan at Panera's. "I was going to suggest Popeye's," Mark said, "But, I didn't want to face celibacy for some fried chicken."

Ted laughed. "We would have been overdressed anyway."

Both men removed their suitcoats. "Well, Ted. Any guess on who did Vincent in." He flipped through a folder. "The tox report didn't reveal anything we didn't already know. A low level of alcohol, but nothing else."

"I was leaning toward Greta Robinson," Ted replied. "But she seems too conniving to just shoot someone." He smiled. "Funny what Mrs. Galley said, about predator and prey. I think Greta's a predator, but maybe too crafty to do something so obvious."

"Maybe she hired someone," Mark said.

"Could be," Ted said. "But we still don't have a motive."

Mark walked to the window. "I still think it's someone from the casino. Whoever did it, seemed to find just the right time and place to shoot Vincent without being detected."

Ted nodded. "And Herb Pine was shot at the same way. Like the perp knew when, where, and how to pull this off."

"Ok, let's get a list of everyone on duty, day and night shift, on the day of both shootings. We start at the top and work our way down the org chart."

CHAPTER 11

(Wednesday the 22nd)

Leona Galley unlocked the front door of Harbor Florists, rolled up the shade, and flicked the lights. She kept the *CLOSED* sign in place. Walking to the register, she logged in and read the message of the day options destined to scroll across the neon banner in the window.

She chose *Override* to bypass the sappy *Say it with Flowers* slogan. A screen opened for her input. *Hmmm, what says 'today,'* she wondered. She walked to the display window and looked across the street to the Long Harbor police station. Mark was sitting in his brightly lit third floor office, back to the window, but clearly enjoying something no doubt bad for him.

She returned to her screen, typed *Surprise Them with Dahlias,* hit *Enter,* and walked to the door, switching the *OPEN* sign to face out to the street.

Mark crumpled the wrapper of his now consumed Bacon, Egg, and Cheese McGriddle and launched a three-pointer toward his metal wastebasket. It clanked off. *I'll pick it up later. I am getting closer.* He sipped his large coffee and pivoted on his rolling chair to look out onto the Long Harbor morning: mountains in the distance, the waterfront off to his right, cars and busses mostly obeying the traffic signals, and the florist shop, open for business.

He reads the neon banner: *Surprise Them with Dahlias.* He gagged on his drink. *Man, she doesn't pull any punches. I hope she sticks with flowers and allows Cupid to pierce hearts. Less drama for this small town.*

•   •   •   •   •

Ted left his car, straightened his tie, and walked to the steps in front of the station. He bound up two at a time, opened the door, and saluted the desk officer. He decided to skip the elevator and run up the polished stairs to the third floor.

"Morning, Chief," he called out as Mark sat rocking in his chair. "I'll line up the interviews at Dirty Sam's. I have a good feeling that we'll make progress on Vincent's death today." He smiled. "The Long Harbor police always gets their man."

Mark motioned Ted over. "Check out the banner at Harbor Florists."

"Surprise Them with Dahlias," Ted said. "Very subtle."

The door of the shop opened. Leona walked out and signaled to the owner of a food cart. He poured a cup of coffee, then pulling some metal wrap, assembled her morning breakfast. Leona handed cash over and received the coffee and meal. She opened the wrapping and sniffed.

She saw Mark and Ted at the window, waved, and lifted the meal toward the men. Meat on a pointed stick. She seemed to mouth something to the men.

"What did she say?" asked Ted.

Mark sighed. "Predator and Prey."

•   •   •   •   •

Herb rode in alone and parked two rows over from the security door. He walked to the elevators, checked the time, and waited as a door dinged and opened. He entered and smiled to a couple holding shopping bags with Dirty Sam's emblazed on the front. The woman reached into her bag and pulled a picture of a feline. "I got a good feeling about the all-day slot tournament today, dear. With Elspeth's help, we're going to take Dirty Sam's for a bundle."

The woman turned the picture toward Herb. "My tabby, Elspeth. It's Scottish and means 'Pledged to God.' Found it in the street as a kitten. Had a broken leg, probably run over. She's our good luck charm now."

The husband rolled his eyes. "Damn, expensive cat, I'd say. Shots, food, litter. It better pay off soon."

The woman threw an elbow into his midsection. "I don't complain about how much you cost me. And Elspeth doesn't snore." She hugged the picture. "Elspeth, just make sure that Ike and Betty don't ruin our day. I couldn't stand losing to that witch."

The elevator stopped at the casino level. Herb waited as the couple left, then followed, watching as they headed to a small room. "Ike and Betty, good to see you today. Ready to come in second?" the woman said to a couple. She sat at the next slot and pulled out Elspeth's picture.

Betty, Herb assumed, returned a Cheshire cat grin and pulled a small doll with a tuft of orange hair from her own bag. "Little Donald is ready for action, Lois. Prepare to face defeat." The husbands shrugged at each other.

A cocktail waitress arrived in the nick of time. "A Whiskey Sour for me, dearie," Lois said. "And don't get cheap on the booze."

Betty patted the waitress's hand. "Please excuse her, young lady." She made a drinking gesture. "She has an issue."

Lois started to say something, but stopped when Charlie signaled her to let it go.

"I'll just have a Diet Coke myself," Betty continued. "Oh, and throw a little rum in there too."

•　　　•　　　•　　　•　　　•

Shirley roared in, picked a spot a row over from Herb, and tied her Harley to a support post. She walked toward the security door, texted Larry, and waited. Minutes later, he opened the door, smiled, and gestured her in. He stopped at a storage closet, bowed to his new girlfriend, and opened the door. A small cot was set up, with flowers sitting atop a chemical container.

He locked the door and embraced Shirley. She squirmed. "Whoa, Larry. We have a big day planned. Do you think this is wise?"

"I had to have you, my little werewolf. Your scent drives me wild."

"Are you sure it's not the industrial strength cleanser sitting next to us?"

Larry smiled and picked up the vase. "I got these for you from the local flower shop. Aren't they pretty?"

Shirley touched one of the flowers. "Yeah, Larry. They're nice."

"I haven't seen these before. Do you know what they're called?" Larry said.

Shirley put the vase back on the metal barrel. "Yes, they're dahlias."

Larry beamed. "Yes, red dahlias. The saleswoman said they brighten up any day."

•　　　•　　　•　　　•　　　•

Greta drove in, circled the parking level once, saw Herb and Shirley's cycles and drove nearer to the security door. She located the two closest cameras and walked to a spot out of current view of both. *This will do just fine.*

She took the elevator to the casino level, walked out, and headed toward the room holding the slot tournament. Larry walked past, head down. "Larry," she called out. "You look like you've been busy. Your shirt is half hanging out and your hair needs combing."

"I just got back from my break," he said. "I lost track of time and had to rush back."

Greta nodded southward. "You're fly's open, Larry. Straighten up for Pete's sake."

Shouting came from the tournament room. The managers walked over and watched the scene taking place. "You and your troll are going down today, Betty. Your orange buddy will meet the defeat he should have had in November."

Betty shook Little Donald at her. "Lois, you, Charlie, and your mangy cat will taste defeat today, just like your crooked friend in the election."

The women stepped nose-to-nose and growled. Each husband stepped in and pulled his wife away. The women signaled for more alcohol.

The hostess awaited instructions from Larry and Greta, who both nodded. She shrugged and took the drink orders. As she walked away, she whispered "They're both half lit already. I hope you know what you're doing."

"I know," both Larry and Greta responded.

•　　　•　　　•　　　•　　　•

Herb paid for his Caramel Macchiato and scanned the Starbucks, already filling with customers. He walked to Shirley's table. "Is this seat taken, miss?"

"It's all yours, sir."

Herb took a sip. "Aaaahhhh," he said. "Nothing like a Macchiato to start your day." He raised his cup again to repeat the experience.

Shirley smiled. "You have me there. My day started by giving Larry a blow job."

Herb spit the hot drink and coughed. A woman sitting nearby

jumped up, hurried behind him, and started to slap him in the back. Herb signaled he was ok. "Too hot to handle, ma'am, he said. "Have to take things slow, I guess."

The woman returned to her table as Herb wiped his mouth, then the table. "Geez, Shirley, couldn't you have just kissed him?"

"He bought me flowers, Herb. What's a girl to do?" She opened her purse and pulled a flower.

"Shit, a dahlia," said Herb. "Now that's a bad sign."

•　　　•　　　•　　　•　　　•

Ted walked into the casino, spotted Phil dealing to a half-filled baccarat table and sighed. *Nope. Have to do my job. He gazed at the glass partition overlooking the floor. Big brother may be watching, anyway.*

He flashed his badge to the guard at the entrance to the manager's area, and walked with him up the stairs to the observation level, deciding to skip the elevator. The guard led Ted to the corner office and started to knock. "That's ok, pal," Ted said. "I'll take it from here."

He walked in as Greta and Larry appeared to be arguing. "What I do on my own time is my business, Greta. You don't seem to be too discrete yourself, flirting with anyone with a dick."

"You didn't mind when it was your dick."

"Ahem," Ted coughed.

The pair turned to Ted, switched to smiles, and welcomed their guest. "Detective Hanson," Larry said. "We didn't expect you today."

Ted smiled. "Apparently not." He walked to the observation window. "We're interviewing all employees on duty around the time of Vincent's death."

"What exactly are you looking *for?*" Greta said. "Do you think an employee killed him?"

"We're looking at all angles." Ted walked to the door and motioned to Larry. "Greta, you're first. Mr. Harkins, if you would excuse us."

• • • • •

Mark strolled through the food court. *I shouldn't have stuck this whole investigation on Ted. It's all hands on deck.* He stopped short after passing the Starbucks. *Well, well.* He walked to the counter, waving to Herb and Shirley as he passed by. "Funny seeing you folks here. Let me get a Venti and I'll join you."

He returned, holding coffee, a dozen sugar packets, and a biscotti. He studied Herb's drink. "What's that?" he asked as he placed his purchases on the small section of table not occupied by the pair. He turned to the woman who had rescued Herb. "Mind if I grab this extra chair?"

She nodded. "Be my guest, young man." She smiled. "Just be careful with your drink. Your friend nearly choked earlier."

Mark glanced at Herb who was whispering something to Shirley. "Do tell. I hope he's ok."

The woman smiled. "I think so. I pounded him on the back a few times and he seemed to clear up." She leaned forward. "That's one hairy guy. It was like pounding on Bigfoot, not a patron of Dirty Sam's."

Mark smiled. "I guess they attract all types here."

He slid the chair to Herb and Shirley's small table. "That kind lady just told me she saved you from choking. Something go down the wrong pipe."

Herb frowned at Shirley. "I guess it happens sometimes."

• • • • •

Greta closed the blinds, sat in the guest chair and crossed her legs. Ted turned from the observation window and sat in the manager's chair, opened his notebook, and clicked his pen. Greta switched leg position, making sure to delay just enough in the middle to get Ted's attention.

Ted clicked his ballpoint, involuntarily, then pulled his phone. "Just texting my *girlfriend* about dinner tonight."

Greta smiled and licked her lips. Ted misspelled 'dinner,' and hit the send arrow.

"Now, Miss Robinson, where were you when Vincent was shot, Sunday the twelfth, ten o'clock or so."

Greta pouted. Ted jumped when his phone chimed. "Let me just check this."

Where for 'sinner'? What do you mean?

Ted read his message: *Where for sinner tonight?* He smiled at Greta. "La Primavera. Good place." He typed *dinner, 7 p.m.*

He put his phone away. "Now, where were you around ten p.m., Sunday the twelfth?"

Greta thought this over. "I was on my shift. I take my break around then." She smiled. "I believe I was entertaining a high roller."

"Can someone corroborate this?"

Greta laughed. "I'm afraid not. Wives or *girlfriends*, you know." She crossed her legs again.

His phone dinged. Greta nodded. "I think your pants are trying to tell you something."

Ted pulled his phone and read the text. *Ok.*

"Do you own a gun, Miss Robinson?"

"I do. A nine millimeter. I carry it for protection. You can't be too careful around here."

"Do you carry during your shift?"

Greta laughed. "No. The owners frown on that. I keep it handy and check on it during my breaks."

"Can we look your gun over?"

"Sorry, detective. It was stolen."

"I see. Stolen from where?"

"The employee locker room. Do you think it was used to shoot Vincent?"

Ted closed his notebook. "We're looking at all angles."

• • • • •

Mark left Herb and Shirley and headed for the gaming area—bright lights, cigarette smoke, cheering seniors pointing to payouts. He walked through the rows of slots, intermingled with gaming tables. He looked for Ted. Nowhere to be found. He glanced at the observation area. *I hope he's sticking to his assignment. Can't have your lead detective shooting craps or hitting on a blackjack hand while he's supposed to be interviewing persons of interest in a murder investigation.*

"Hi, Jennie. Room for another player?"

Mark turned at the sound of the voice. Professor Jim Cooper. *Doesn't he ever teach?* Mark ambled over. *I wonder what he knows.*

A shrill voice. "James Cooper! Get away from that table. You have a job to get to."

Jim lowered his head, turned without looking at the other players, and met his wife. "Jan, just playing a few hands before work."

She sneered at him, then at Jennie, then the other players. Heads bowed. *Maybe she'll take her husband and go away.*

Jennie pulled back Jim's cards then pushed his bet toward him. "Your chips. Mr. Cooper."

He accepted his currency and fate. He stood and walked steps behind his wife toward the exit. Other gamblers avoided eye contact. No one wants their spouse to drag them from a hot table.

Mark pitied Jim. *Poor schnook. He's overmatched. Maybe it's for the better.*

He saw Jim walk past Herb, Shirley, and Larry. They appeared to have been talking. Jan stopped, turned and started to say something to the threesome. Jim put his arm around her shoulder. "Let's just leave," he whispered.

Greta walked up to Larry. "You're next, Larry. Hanson's on the warpath."

Larry walked past Mark, not noticing him. Mark went over to the three. "Well, Herb, looks like your friend Jim won't be around here much longer."

Herb glanced to the retreating ex-priest, being led away by his wife. "All for the best, I guess."

"He didn't cash his chips," Mark said.

"Oh, He'll be back. He's in too deep."

•　　•　　•　　•　　•

Ted opened the blinds and waved Larry to the guest chair. "So, Larry. Where were you on Sunday the twelfth when Vincent was shot? You managed the first shift that day."

"I hung around and took in the Jeff Dunham show." He smiled. "One of the perks of the job." He snorted. "And I love Achmed the dead terrorist."

Ted made a note. "When did the show let out?"

"Nine-thirty. Not too many late night shows in this casino on Sunday nights.

"Vincent died around that time. What did you do when the show let out?"

Larry scratched his chin. "Roamed around. Scrounged a drink from The Golden Ore, went home."

"Can anyone vouch for you at that time?"

"No. I got home around eleven-thirty and went to bed. I had an early day Monday."

Ted closed his notebook. "Do you own a gun, Larry?"

"No. I should, I guess. You never know when you'll need it in this business."

•　　•　　•　　•　　•

Mark left Herb and Shirley and wound his way to the security door. Turning to get his bearings, he realized he was at the back of a large room holding dozens of seniors, madly pressing buttons, shaking their fists at their neighbors, and hooting. A bell rang and the players reached for drinks.

"End of round one," a man in a tuxedo said. "We'll tally the scores and announce the standings when you get back from your lunch. Two p.m. sharp."

A woman lifted a tiny doll, which had a tuft of bright orange hair. She pointed it at another woman and said something indecipherable but mean enough to have those nearby turn toward her.

Her nemesis flashed a photo, twitched her hips, and danced out of the room. Two men, Mark assumed they were the husbands, shrugged, and followed their wives out.

"That's a slot tournament, Chief," said Carla, causing Mark to jump. "Mostly seniors, pumped up by Kahlua, and hopes of hitting it big. They kick in a hundred bucks to buy in, and can win a couple grand if the wheels turn their way."

"Carla, aren't you a waitress?"

"Yeah, but I'm picking up shift work today as a cocktail hostess. Need the money."

Mark turned toward the tournament area. "Arguing, yelling, and shaking dolls at opponents. Doesn't seem like much fun."

Carla laughed. "Fun they can get watching their grandkids. This is serious business to them. They bring their trolls, prayer cards, and pet pictures, anything for an edge." She pointed to a scoreboard displaying totals for the top players. "This is the tournament they look forward to. Big bucks and lots of slot junkies. It can get pretty hectic, especially around five when the last round completes."

She placed an empty glass on her tray. "They're given an hour for lunch so they can sober up, and we can clean up after them. Hopefully, no one's crapped themselves." She laughed. "Sometimes they have to replace a chair if it's really bad."

"Oh, miss," a man called out.

"Have to get back to work, Mark. Steer clear of these folks if you can. They can get pretty rowdy and disrupt an otherwise quiet day."

•　　　•　　　•　　　•　　　•

LaVonne sat in the employee locker room and checked her phone. A text message from dad. *Let's meet for dinner. I'm buying.* She typed: *Working an extra shift at Dirty Sam's to pick up some cash. We can meet in the food court around five.*

A quick ding. *Ok* and a smiley face.

A cocktail hostess walked in, grabbed cigarettes from her locker, and pointed in the direction of the gaming area. "Boy, the slot tournament is crazier than usual. Two ladies are close to punching each other out. They're on the lunch break now. I hope they sober up." She started toward the back door. "Tell Manny that you guys may need to help bust up fights later on."

LaVonne stood, checked herself in the mirror, adjusted her cap, and started toward the same door. Once outside, she saw the hostess leaning against the wall. "You really shouldn't be using this door, Jill. This is only for security." LaVonne accepted a cigarette from her.

Jill flicked her smoke. "You know, LaVonne, when we finished high school just a few years ago, who knew we'd be puffing away in a desolate corner of Dirty Sam's, and wondering what's happened to us."

LaVonne laughed. "We're both just waiting for our big break, Jill. When things happen for us, they'll happen fast."

She stamped out the cigarette, nodded to Jill and walked away. Swinging her flashlight in a wide arc, she scanned for suspicious activity, and hoped there was none to be found on this otherwise typical Wednesday.

A few rows over, she spotted a Harley chained to a stanchion. *Herb Pine must be here.* On the next row, another Hog. A pink streamer hung from the handlebar. *Another cyclist. Don't recognize this one. Decked out like Herb's. I wonder if they know each other.*

She recorded her position in her log, then, making sure no one was in sight, mounted the bike. She place her feet on the pedals. "Vroom, vroom," she whispered.

"Don't forget to start it first," Shirley called out. "Otherwise, you'll just sit there."

LaVonne turned red when she saw her. "Sorry, ma'am. Must seem childish of me."

Shirley smiled. "Not at all, young lady. Go for it." She pointed to the switches on the handlebar. "Do you know how to start one of these babies?"

"I do," LaVonne said. "My ex-boyfriend had one."

"Give it a spin—" She read LaVonne's nametag. "Miss Wilson."

"I really shouldn't. I'm on duty."

"It will be our secret. Take life by the horns." Shirley opened the luggage rack and pulled her helmet. "Try this on."

LaVonne strapped on the black helmet. "You look like the real thing, LaVonne," Shirley said. "Take a lap or two around the level."

LaVonne started the Hog, inched out, and, after a nod from Shirley, drove down the lane. Picking up speed, she headed three rows over, turned, and drove past the elevator, slowing as she passed Jill. LaVonne tapped the horn and continued off.

"You go, girl," Jill shouted. "Make it happen."

•   •   •   •   •

Ted started working his way down the employee list. The dealers were more likely to know Vincent, so he concentrated on them. Phil walked into the manager's office and sat when Ted pointed to the chair.

"So Phil, where were you Sunday the twelfth, around ten when Vincent was shot?"

Phil hesitated and sighed. "I was in the Golden Ore Lounge, waiting for my date to show up."

"Can she verify this?"

He frowned. "No, she stood me up. I should have known better. That Greta's one crazy bitch."

"You were dating Greta?"

"She came on to me." He laughed. "Like she does with half the men in this place. Phil sat forward. "Hey, I saw you with her last week."

"Just a quick conversation, Phil," Ted hurried, then clicked his pen repeatedly. "I didn't know she was dating Vincent."

"Big time." Phil smiled. "Though I got the impression she was playing him for a schnook." He swung the chair looking at the door for any possible bystander. "She'll screw her way around until she gets what she wants."

$\bullet \qquad \bullet \qquad \bullet \qquad \bullet \qquad \bullet$

Mark decided to remain at Dirty Sam's for the afternoon. *Too many people of interest here for a weekday. May be nothing, but worth observing for a little while, at least. Plus I want to see how that slot tournament goes.*

He walked past a blackjack table. Herb was playing, but seemed disinterested, having to be asked by the dealer if he wanted to hit or stay. Mark patted him on the shoulder, causing Herb to flinch as he turned. "Mark, still here?"

"Yep. We're intensifying our investigation of Vincent's killing. Who knows, maybe we'll also find the guy who shot at you."

"I can handle myself, Chief. He *or she* owes me a windshield and an explanation."

Mark nodded. "Enjoy yourself here, Herb." He turned to look for Shirley. "Where's your old lady? I might as well wish her luck also."

Mark smiled. "There she is. Seems a bit distracted. Oh, Larry's coming over to talk to her. I think I'll join them." Mark walked over to the pair, who stopped talking when they saw him.

Herb cashed his chips and walked to the cashier cage. Mark turned from Larry and Shirley and pointed to the blackjack table. He scanned the surrounding area, saw Herb, and waved. Herb nodded, lifted his chips, and pointed to the cashier's. He turned in time to walk into Betty.

Betty opened her purse and pulled mace. "Betty, wait, it's the man we met in the elevator," said Ike, sparing Herb from a chemical assault.

"Sorry, young man. You can't be too careful here," she said. "People get crazy when there's money involved."

Ike put his hand on her shoulder. "Let's get back to the tournament, Betty. We should get settled, and I'm sure our friend has something to do also." He turned to Herb. "Good luck today, young man." He smiled. "Leave some money for us, though."

●　　　　●　　　　●　　　　●　　　　●

The slot players chatted, combed their trolls, and checked their smart phones one last time. Betty performed a slow, menacing Tai Chi meant to relax her button tapping muscles as well as intimidate Lois, who pretended to ignore this as she crocheted a small square of thick cloth. She clicked the needles loud enough to disturb Betty's Zen, and hummed. The husbands discussed baseball and compared their picks for the weekend games.

The MC nodded to both couples as he walked in. *Three more hours of this, and I can get paid and drive off to my magic gig at Birds of a Feather. Nothing like pulling a scarf from a G-string.*

He smiled to himself. *Larry was right. Maybe I can try some tricks out on these folks. Maybe a grand finale when the tournament had ended.* He studied the crowd. *I don't see a lovely assistant, but maybe one of these goofy women will do. I'm sure the husband would love her to disappear.* He pulled his pocket watch: 2 p.m. "Time for round two folks," he shouted. "Please return to your seats, put your smart phones away, aaaannnnnnddddd get ready to rumble."

CHAPTER 12

LaVonne checked her watch: 3:00. Come on, Mickey, let's get this day moving. A Jeep turned into the lane and swung into a slot 50 yards away. Leona Galley got out, slammed the door, and walked up to LaVonne. She stopped, opened her purse, and removed a cone-shaped object wrapped in tissue paper.

"Good afternoon, Miss Wilson. I left my shop early today. Things were slow and my assistant offered to cover for me. We have a special today." She offered the paper to LaVonne, who opened the gift. "It's a red dahlia. Enjoy."

"Thanks, Mrs. Galley, but I have nowhere to put it."

Leona raised a finger. "One moment." She opened her purse, removed a small scissors and a safety pin, took the flower, and snipped away most of the base. She worked the flower into LaVonne's lapel, securing it with the pin.

She took a step back. "There you are. The most stylish guard at Dirty Sam's."

LaVonne sniffed the dahlia. "Thanks again."

"Dahlias rarely have a scent, LaVonne," Leona said. "But they have medicinal purposes and are said to lead one to romance."

"It's gotta beat Tinder," LaVonne said, smiling.

"How's that father of yours? I imagine he's a ladies man. So strong and handsome."

LaVonne sighed. "He's kept to himself once mom died." She brushed the flower. "I'm seeing him on my break at five. I'll let him know you were asking for him."

"Thanks, my dear. Well, I must be on my way. I'm meeting friends myself today."

"Enjoy your visit, Mrs. Galley," LaVonne replied.

"Oh I will, dearie. It will be nice to catch up with old acquaintances."

• • • • •

Mark and Ted met up at 3:30. They walked to Dirty Subs and ordered. Mark took his mushroom cheesesteak, dirty fries, and bottled water to a clean table. Ted followed with a chef salad and bottle of diet Iced Tea.

"Mark, no 64-ounce soda?"

The chief shook his head. "I'll be in trouble enough for the cheesesteak and fries. Have to tell Linda I took *some* steps to be healthy."

Ted opened his notebook. "The missing gun seems to be the problem. Greta said her nine millimeter was stolen. No one else fesses up to even owning one."

"And you believe her?"

"She agreed to have a patrolman inspect her locker. Nothing there."

Mark bit off a chunk of his sandwich, took a few seconds to swallow, and then wiped his mouth with a half dozen napkins. "Damn, that's good." He opened his water, took a sip, and winced. "This would go better with a high sugar drink." He shook his head. "The things we do for love."

He worked a dozen fries into his mouth. "Mmmmmppppphhhh, mmmmmpppppphhhh, Ted," Mark mumbled.

"Sorry, Mark. I didn't get that."

Mark swallowed, drained half the bottle of water, and then sat back. "How about a motive. What's common to Vincent and Herb?"

"Besides the gambling, I'm not sure." Ted laughed. "Though they were both probably screwing Greta."

"A jealous boyfriend?"

"Or someone who imagined he was the boyfriend." Ted said. "I don't think Greta is the boyfriend type. She seems to keep all options open."

Mark tossed his napkin on the paper plate. "I give up. I'm no match for Dirty Subs."

A shadow came over the men. "Chief Porfino and Detective Hanson. Fancy seeing you here."

Ted stood as Mark turned. "Leona. Well, everyone is here today. Care to join us?"

"You can stay seated, gentlemen. I can't stay. I'm late meeting Carla." She smiled. "We've become fast friends."

Leona turned and then stopped. "And here's the mayor. Yoo-hoo, Mr. Mayor, come on over."

Leona. Crap. Didn't expect to see her. And my chief of police and lead detective. He waved and walked over. "Hello all. Just meeting my daughter on her dinner break. It's at five but I figured I'd roam around and take things in." He nodded to those constituents who recognized him. "Anything hopping today?"

"There's a slots tournament, which looks like it could turn interesting," Mark said. "Though, I'm not sure Fallujah prepared you for drunken seniors wielding trolls and cat pictures."

"I'll have to check it out later," Evers said. "I'll keep my distance to avoid direct fire."

Mark collected his trash and stood. Ted followed. "We have to be off to check on a few things," Mark said to Leona and Evers.

Ted whispered to Mark. "It's a small world, I guess, seeing those two today."

Mark nodded. "But somehow, they seem like old acquaintances."

• • • • •

Betty stabbed at the play button. "Hit, you Mother."

Ike looked over. "Really, Betty. It's just a dumb machine. It produces random combinations."

"Eyes to yourself, Ike Sanders. If you want to share in my winnings, you'll keep your opinions to yourself."

"And don't forget she's bat-shit crazy, Ike," Lois called over as she stabbed away without looking up.

The MC called out. "Ten more minutes for this round folks. Then the bonus round. It's anyone's game to win."

Charley waved to Ike. The men stood. "Wanna grab a quick drink at the Golden Ore?"

"Lead the way, buddy," said Ike. "There's no way this ends well."

They left the tournament room. "Boy, that was intense," Ike said. "And the cigarette smoke. Some of those women don't bother with an ash tray. Just let it fall in their laps."

The Golden Ore was almost empty. The men walked in and sat at the bar. "I'll have a Heineken," Charley called out to the bartender. "And my friend will have..." Charlie looked at his friend.

"I'll have a Flying Fish," Ike replied. "And Barkeep, a fresh bowl of beer nuts."

At a corner table, Herb nudged Shirley. "The husbands. We gotta get them back to their wives. It's getting close to five."

"Chill, Herb," Shirley said. "There's still time. Let them get liquored up. The drunker, the merrier."

• • • • •

Mark stopped and sat at a Simpsons slot. He pointed to the next chair and Ted slid onto the cushioned pleather. "Are we gambling today, Boss?"

"Just a little, Ted. This gives us a good view of the security door. Let's see who goes in and out. I'd like to see who uses it."

Ted nodded toward the tournament room. "And it gives us front row seats to the real action. Look, there's those crazy women. They look ready to fight."

"Hmmm," Mark said. "And the husbands are gone. No safety valve."

He deposited $10 and spun. "Well, Ted. If we don't catch a murderer today, maybe we can at least quell a civil uprising."

Leona Galley walked by. "Oh, my. Law enforcement playing slots in the middle of Sodom."

Mark waved her to the third Simpson's seat. "Join us, Leona. This is a study in human nature, and greed."

Leona sat and pulled a hundred from her purse. "I only see prey waiting to be relieved of their hides."

The three turned to the slots room as they heard, "Come on, you Mother, and give mama a big win." Lois shook her fist at Betty and shushed her.

"The forest is full of strange and wonderful creatures, gentlemen. Yet, they all contribute to the eco system, and to the inevitable climax of the battle between predator and prey."

Ike and Charley walked by holding their beers. They entered the slot room and positioned themselves next to their wives, who ignored them as they stabbed away. "And there are the mates, accepting the conflict, and hoping to escape unharmed."

•   •   •   •   •

Larry stood at the observation window and took in the activity below. *A normal day so far. Except for those lunatics in the slot room.* He smiled. *Little do you know, folks, that you'll be part of Dirty Sam's history...and have a front row seat to our own little Ocean's Eleven.*

"Larry, you look like you're daydreaming. What's up?"

He turned to the night manager, then nodded to the gaming area. "The usual suspects, gambling their way out of their disposable cash."

Greta laughed. "Well, I'm sure the money will go to a good cause." She pointed. "Hey, look. Mark Porfino and Ted Hanson sitting at a Simpsons slot." She leaned closer. "And that's Leona Galley."

They both eyed the clock in the room: 4:30.

●　　　●　　　●　　　●　　　●

Lenny and Walt talked football as their Brinks truck fought rush-hour traffic. "This is the Predators year, Lenny," said Walt. "I can feel it. Good quarterback, good defense, a kicker who never misses. The preseason should be fun."

Lenny shook his head. "Never bet against the Patriots, Walt. They're always there at the end and they get better as the season goes on." He pressed his walkie-talkie. "Hey Robby, Who's better, the Pats, or the Predators?"

Robby stretched his legs in the back of the van and switched on his radio. "I really don't care, guys. I'd rather talk about *Guys and Dolls* coming to the Harbor Fine Arts Center."

Lenny smirked and winked at Walt. "Oh, the Farts Center." The men stifled their laughs.

"Very funny, guys. You could stand some culture."

"We're not rich enough for culture, Robby," said Walt.

Robby chuckled. "We'll have a shitload of cash in just a few minutes."

"Don't even joke about that, Robby," Lenny said.

"Just thinking out loud guys. A couple hundred grand, split three ways. That buys a lot of football tickets, or a getaway to Cancun." He chuckled. "Don't tell me you never thought about it."

"Thinking is bad for you, Robby. We pick up the cash, deliver it, and hold onto our boring, steady jobs."

"Ok, guys. Loud and clear." He turned off his two-way. *Lenny's right. Nothing exciting ever happens in this job.*

•   •   •   •   •

Evers nursed a coffee, and waited for LaVonne. An elderly couple walked by, the wife holding a cloth bag with a stuffed dog trying to climb out. He smiled. *People and their addictions. Rushing to bring their money to a heartless, soulless gambling den, hoping to beat them at their own game. The house always wins, folks. Save your money.*

A counter clerk, barely out of his teens from what Evers could tell, came over and started to clean a nearby table. A young female walked over and said, "Billy, did you hear the slots tournament is getting nasty. Two ladies are yelling at each other and waving trolls and cat pictures at each other."

"I just hope they stay outta here. Those folks make a mess, treat us like we're their ungrateful grandchildren if we don't fawn over them, and complain about everything." He put down his spray bottle. "Wait a minute. Does one of them have a troll with wild orange hair?"

"That's what I heard."

"Crap. That's my grandmother. This is gonna be a bad day."

Evers dumped the cup into the bin, and walked toward the gaming area. *I still have a few minutes. I have to see this.* He passed blackjack tables, penny slots, and video poker machines. He followed the noise. He stopped when he saw Mark, Ted, and Leona Galley sitting at slots, and pointing to the tournament area.

Farther down the polished walkway, he saw Herb Pine and his hairy girlfriend slide into chairs at a baccarat table.

A man in a cheap tux and holding a mic, called out from the

tournament room. "Ok, folks, the Frenzy Faceoff. We're down to four spinners. Betty, Lois, Mitzy, and Vera. You're all guaranteed a cash prize, ladies. But let's see who qualifies for a shot at the grand prize of ten thousaaaaaaddddd dollarsssss."

The survivors, and those vanquished in the previous rounds, all cheered. Gamblers at tables and slots outside the area continued to gamble, but also watched and listened.

Evers checked his watch. "I'm afraid I have to miss this," he said to Mark and his companions. "Meeting my daughter at five." He walked off toward the food court.

"I guess I should go, too," Mark said. "Ted, stick around and watch the security door. Log who comes in and out." He laughed. "And make sure the slots tournament ends without incident. Meet me tomorrow morning and we'll go over where we are."

Leona cashed out. "Let me redeem this, Mark, and I'll follow you to the garage."

Ted sat watching the door.

"Ahem. Are you going to take up that seat all day, son, or give us a chance to clean out Homer Simpson?"

Three ladies, armed with mixed drinks and attitude, stared at Ted. "Don't make us signal for the attendant. If you're done here, vamoose."

Ted cashed out, stood, and pulled his badge. "No need to cause a scene, young ladies." He pointed to the drinks. "How do I know you're old enough for alcohol?"

They laughed. "Do you want to see ID, young man," said the apparent ring leader.

"I'll let you go this time, ladies. Just don't be picking up innocent men. Dirty Sam's is a respectable place."

The women laughed and sat. The first said, "You're cute." The last pinched his ass. Ted wagged a finger at the trio. "I'll be watching you ladies."

•   •   •   •   •

Evers returned to Dirty Subs and saw LaVonne seated at a corner table. "What can I get you, LaVonne?"

"Just a Chicken Caesar and water, Dad. I'm trying to diet."

"Ok, but they have great fries here."

LaVonne passed.

Evers returned a few minutes with his order. "I got a salad, too." He pinched his stomach overhanging his belt. "I have to get back down to my Iraq weight. Who knows when I'll have to take on hostile forces again?" He opened a dressing packet. "Have you seen some of these seniors? The slots tournament itself reeks of danger and intrigue."

They dug into their salads. "So tell me, LaVonne. Seriously. Is Dirty Sam's turning our community into a war zone?" He snatched a crouton which had rolled across the table. "This used to be a quiet casino, catering to busses of gamblers holding meal vouchers. Now there's a killing, attempted murder, who knows what else."

He saw Mark walking out with Leona. "There goes the chief of police, and an old friend of mine. I wonder if she's part of all this"

LaVonne turned to the pair. "Mrs. Galley? Why she wouldn't hurt a fly."

"You'd be surprised."

•   •   •   •   •

The MC signaled the last break before the sudden-death round. "Ten minutes to pee, relax, order a drink, and get ready for the finale." He pointed to the scoreboard. "Still neck and neck. It's down to Betty and Lois."

The woman stood and stretched. The husbands hurried off toward the Men's room. "Weaklings," Betty said nodding to the retreating spouses. She sipped her Kahlua. "A stiff drink, and a good pair of Depends. I'm ready for the final battle."

Lois brushed off her picture of Elspeth, sipped her Whiskey Sour, and sat back. "I'm getting too old for this, Betty. Let's ditch the husbands and slip off to Birds of a Feather later on. The guys will be napping by seven anyway."

"You're on, sister. Let me just finish kicking your ass."

Lois glanced at Elspeth. "What a turd...right my love?" She turned to Betty. "Prepare for one serious ass-whooping."

The MC checked his gear. "Smoke, igniter, cloak. Ready," he whispered. He saw the women arguing. *People will be glad to see an old lady disappear.*

He took a sip of his coffee. In just a few minutes, Murray the Magnificent will be famous at Dirty Sam's.

•   •   •   •   •

LaVonne hugged her father and returned to the employee's room. She put her leftovers in the refrigerator, flipped open a compact mirror, and smiled. She scratched off the piece of lettuce that had stuck to her front teeth. *Better. Now back to the garage.*

She heard cheering. *The slot tournament must be finishing up.* She logged her position and walked into the parking level. A Brinks truck turned down the row. LaVonne checked with Mickey. A few minutes after five, the evening pickup.

The truck headed to the security door. She nodded to the driver and his companion and turned to the door. Larry came out and waved to the men. LaVonne recorded the time and walked further down the row of cars away from the truck.

Lenny and Walt jumped out, walked to the back, and opened the secured doors. Robby climbed out and stood rigid. He nodded to the men to follow Larry inside. After they were out of sight, Shirley stepped up from behind, and held a chloroformed towel to Robby's face as he turned to her. He toppled within a few seconds.

Shirley dragged the man behind a pickup, returned to the truck and climbed inside, closing the door. *Part one complete.*

•　　　•　　　•　　　•　　　•

Murray the Magnificent signaled Betty to come up on the stage. He positioned her next to him, and lifted her arm. "Ladies and Gentlemen, the winner of today's tournament and ten thousand dollars..." He whispered to her and signaled to the mic. "Betty Goldstein, G-O-L-D-S-T-E-I-N," she shouted. The crowd applauded, even Lois. Murray whispered something else to her. She frowned. He cupped his hand, leaned forward and spoke to her again, his hand hiding any dialog from the crowd. She glanced down, smiled, and nodded.

Two hostesses carrying a large cardboard check walked up with a man in a dark suit. The man took the mic from Murray. "Hi, folks," he said. "I'm Benny Watson, General Manager of Dirty Sam's." He took out a Sharpie and wrote *Betty Goldstein* on the "Pay to" line.

He had each hostess hold an end of the check, and then handed the mic back to Murray, who he positioned next to Betty. Benny stepped next to one of the hostesses and signaled to a photographer. The man stepped in front of the group, had everyone skootch just a little bit closer, and lifted his camera. "Smile and say moneeeyyyyy," he called out. A series of flashes captured the moment.

Murray stepped forward. "And now folks, for a special surprise, Mrs. Goldstein will disappear." A hush from all present. Betty winked at Ike and smiled, Ike stared at Benny, and the hostesses shrugged at each other. Murray pulled a wand, and checked the igniter. "Disappear, Betty Goldstein!" he said. He pointed the short black rod at Betty, flicked the igniter, and a gust of smoke enveloped the woman. When the smoke cleared, Betty was missing. The crown gasped, then cheered.

• • • • •

Ted watched the tournament proceedings, while also following Larry, Walt, and Lenny as they walked toward the security door with a dolly holding today's take. The men opened the door, but stopped as they heard a poof and applause. Larry hurried the guards to continue out the door, which he closed behind him.

A hairy hand placed a chloroform rag over Lenny's mouth, while Larry stopped and turned to Walt. Greta stood after crouching behind an Explorer. She pulled a rag and covered Walt's nose and mouth. She then took the dolly as Walt collapsed.

Larry hadn't expected this. *Why is Greta here?* "Larry, don't stand there all day. This thing is heavy," Greta shouted. Larry helped Greta roll the dolly toward the truck. He opened the door, and was met with his own chloroform, this time from Shirley.

Ted stood from his slot when he saw the smoke, and rushed to the stage, looking over at the security door, which had closed. He flashed his badge to Benny, and waved through the smoke. No Betty. He pushed the curtain aside. No Betty. "And now, Betty Goldstein will reappear from thin air."

Murray guided Ted away from the curtain. "You'll see better from the front, Detective. Now, everyone repeat after me. Presto, Chango, Betty Goldstein, reappear." The crowd murmured the incantation, still unsure of what was happening. Another shake of the wand, another spark from the igniter. More smoke. When the smoke cleared, Betty stood, waving the smoke away, and holding a fresh Kahlua.

The crown applauded. Ike was non-committal. He missed the peace and quiet of no Betty. Lois walked up to her nemesis. "Where did you go, Betty?"

She smiled. "A magician never reveals her tricks."

Ted checked Betty for any wear and tear. She appeared fine. He walked away shaking his head. *What next?*

•   •   •   •   •

Jim headed to the elevator atrium. The Brinks truck barreled down the lane. Jim ran the last few steps as the truck passed within feet of him. *Man, what was his problem,* he wondered, *hauling out and endangering customers. Must have a lot of money today to be in such a hurry. I wonder what their take is on a typical day. I bet it's more than I make in a year.*

He stopped and followed the truck as it turned toward the exit. Hmm, that driver had his face covered up. So did the guy riding shotgun, though it appeared to be slipping off. Wait a minute. That was Larry Harkins.

He turned to where the truck had been. He saw a white and black pile on the ground. Walking over, he saw arms and legs. He turned each man. *Hey, those are the security guards.*

LaVonne was at the end of the row of cars. Jim jumped up and down and waved his arms. "Miss Wilson, come over here, please," he shouted. "Something bad has happened."

She squinted. "That's Jim Cooper. What's up with him," she whispered. "Ok, sir. I'll be right there," she shouted. She phoned Manny. "Boss, a patron is frantically shouting for me to come over. I might need some backup here."

She put her phone away and hurried toward Jim, who was kneeling at what seemed like a pile of white and black laundry. As she drew near, she shuddered. *Wait a minute, those are bodies. Holy cow. What's happened?* She started to run. *And why does this always occur on my shift?*

She had Jim stand and made sure he was ok. Then she examined the guards. She noticed condensation on the ground. *Where's the truck?*

"Mr. Cooper, what did you see?"

Jim caught his breath, sat on a concrete barrier, and shook his head. "I saw the Brinks trunk go by. Two men in the front. Not sure who else there was."

"Did you recognize the men?"

Jim paused. "Well, I'm not certain about the driver, but in the passenger seat, I could swear it was Larry, the day manager."

"Stay right here," she said as she opened the security door and ran into the casino.

Ted turned his head as he heard "Detective!" LaVonne ran into the slot room. "Detective Hanson, come outside. The Brinks guards are laying on the ground in a heap." She leaned forward to catch her breath. "And their truck is gone."

•   •   •   •   •

Mark took the call from Ted. "Chief, someone just robbed Dirty Sam's. The Brinks truck is missing and the guards are knocked out. LaVonne reported it and is still pretty shaken up. Greta is working with the general manager to determine exactly what happened."

"Where were you at the time?"

"I was watching the security door to see who walked in and out. Then a loud noise came from the tournament room." Ted laughed. "You won't believe this, Chief. The MC is also a magician. He made that loudmouth Betty disappear in front of the crowd. It was pretty amazing."

Mark squeezed a stress ball. "Ted, first things first. You didn't see the robbery, or anything unusual around the security door?"

"No, Chief," said Ted. "I took Murray, that's the MC, aside and asked him why he performed the trick just then." He snorted. "You know what he said..."

Silence on the line. "What, dammit, Ted. What did he say?"

Ted held the phone away from his ear. *Boy, Mark is really pissed.* "He said that Larry suggested it. Said it would give a resounding finish to a successful tournament."

"Is Larry still there, Ted?"

Silence on the line. "Crap, Chief. He's gone. Last time I saw him was before the robbery."

Mark threw the stress ball against the wall. "Well, Ted. I guess we know suspect number one." He put a Girl Scout pecan sandy in his mouth and chomped away.

"Chief, are you there?"

Mark swallowed. "Yeah, Ted. Look, I'll put out an APB. Don't let anyone leave. Lock the doors if you have to." He stood and started to put on his coat. "I'm coming over. Tell Murray he has a lot of explaining to do."

•　　　•　　　•　　　•　　　•

Mark parked and walked toward the security door. Police cars with lights flashing framed the area. Ted waved. "Over here, Mark." He pointed to the men who were wearing blankets and drinking coffee.

Walt stood and took off his blanket. He pulled his phone, called his office, and shook his head. "Man, this is a shit storm. There goes my bonus, and maybe my job and pension."

Lenny and Robby stood. "I need a stiff drink," Lenny said. "Man, one minute I'm carting out money, the next I'm in dreamland. That must be good stuff."

Ted looked at Mark. "Chloroform, I think. They were knocked out quick and without any force. They all said they saw a cloth cover their face, then lights out."

A Lincoln town car pulled around the corner, lights flashed. "Crap, it's Evers," Mark said. "There goes my pension too, I guess."

Evers screeched to a halt, feet from the last police car. He rushed out and speed-walked to Mark. "What's going on, Chief? LaVonne called me. I had just left. Dirty Sam's was robbed?"

Ted stepped forward, "Yes, Mr. Mayor. LaVonne's inside getting some rest and talking to Manny. She called him when she was flagged down by Jim Cooper. He saw the bodies and called out to her."

Evers shook his head. "Boy, is she ever going to need counseling." He waved Jim over. "Hi, Mr. Cooper. I understand you discovered the bodies. Did you see anything else?"

"I saw the Brinks truck drive by. I didn't recognize the driver, but I know who the passenger was."

Mark, Ted, and Evers waited. "It was Larry Harkins, the day manager."

•   •   •   •   •

The men sat in Starbucks and compared notes. "So, this was an inside job, led by Larry Harkins?" asked Evers.

Mark nodded. "I put out an APB for both the truck and Larry." He took a sip of his Macchiato. "I wonder how long he was planning this." He sighed. "He didn't seem like the criminal type. Maybe he was in cahoots with someone who could influence him. Someone who had a sway over him."

Ted grimaced. "Someone like Greta, a major cock tease."

"Greta's working this shift. Have you questioned her?"

Ted shrugged. "Yeah. Just a normal night she said, nothing unusual. The casino GM Benny Watson said the same thing."

Mark crumbled his cup. "Talk to her again, and have Watson there. Go over everything that happened at the end of the slot tournament, everything. Don't mention Larry Harkins yet."

Evers finished his lemon bar, then raised a finger. "And find out how the MC made Betty Goldstein disappear."

•   •   •   •   •

Larry opened his eyes. He was riding in the Brinks truck traveling north on Route 9. He felt the bandana covering his mouth. He pulled it down and glanced at the driver. "Herb Pine," he said. "What the fuck's happening?"

Herb removed his face covering. "You just robbed Dirty Sam's, Larry," he responded. "With unknown accomplices." Herb saw Larry starting to drift. "Get some more shuteye, my friend. We're almost there."

Herb waited for traffic to clear, then drove into the woods, stopping a half mile in. He rapped twice on the truck cabin, jumped out, and joined Shirley, who had come around via the back. She handed him red spray paint from a satchel. The two carefully covered any markings indicating the current commercial use. Shirley opened the bag again and pulled a cardboard lettering sign. *Pinelands Medical Supply.*

Herb reapplied his mask while Shirley took a can of white spray. He taped the sign above where *Brinks* had read. "Ok, Herb," she said. "Watch your hair."

She shot the white paint across the lettering. They hurried to the other side, unfurled a similar sign, and, in a few minutes, had matching business logos. Shirley reached into the bag once more. "Get this, Herb." More lettering. Herb scrunched his eyes trying to translate, then laughed. "Perfect," he said. After applying to the rear door, the couple stood back and admired the art work. *Keep Back 100 yards*, it read.

They walked to the passenger door and pulled Larry out. Shirley applied more chloroform. Herb removed the dolly from the back, placed the day manager on top, strapped him in, and carted their partner in crime deeper into the woods. They opened a small duck blind and rolled him in. Shirley scribbled a note and attached it to Larry's shoes, facing the captive. It read, *Later Alligator.*

• • • • •

Mark walked into the small Lucky Roller office. Murray the Magnificent smiled at him and took a top hat from a nearby seat. He tapped it with his wand. A small, white rabbit appeared. Mark pulled out the animal, felt its respiration, and petted it as he sat. "It's a Dwarf Hotot," Murray said. "Named Mimi. Adorable." He pulled a carrot from his coat pocket and handed it to Mark. "Let him nibble on this and you have a friend forever."

The rabbit pooped into Mark's hand. "That's a sign of affection, Chief. Means she's comfortable with you." Mark let Mimi crawl across the desk while he disposed of the pellets.

"So, Murray the Magnificent, is it?"

Murray nodded. "Part-time master of ceremonies, part-time illusionist. I work the senior circuit, mostly. That, and kids." He leaned forward. "Both are tough crowds. You get the occasional knee in the groin."

"From the kids?"

"Both. I actually wear a cup if the room looks hostile."

Mark smiled. "Maybe I should try that myself." He opened his notepad. "So, Mr. Magnificent..."

"Please, call me Murray, Chief. No need for formality."

"Where'd you get the idea to have someone disappear at the end of the slot tournament? Is this something you do all the time?"

Murray smiled. "I'm always pitching my act. Funny, Larry and Greta weren't interested at first, but then yesterday, Larry comes over and tells me he likes the idea." He smiled. "Fortunately, Dirty Sam's uses the stage for other performance art, so the disappearance was doable." He grabbed Mimi before she could jump off the desk. "All I needed was a willing participant. The Kahlua sealed the deal."

Mark sat back. "Did you see Larry afterwards?"

Murray shook his head. "No, I haven't seen him since my performance. Greta, either. Benny scowled at me, so maybe he didn't know about the trick." He lifted Mimi, put her in the top hat, tapped it with the rod, and said "Away, Mimi." The rabbit disappeared.

Mark nodded. "Very impressive, Murray." He pointed to the man's pocket, which was changing shape. "I hope you have carrots in there. Unless you're wearing a cup."

CHAPTER 13

Leona waited for Herb and Shirley to drive away. She emerged from the bushes, wearing camouflage and smeared with greasepaint. She hoisted the stock pouch for her Ravin R15 onto her shoulder and edged to the hut, staying near the trees. She pushed back the tarp covering the entrance and peered inside. A man was strapped to a dolly, struggling to get loose.

"You look familiar," she said, causing the man to stop squirming. He said something muffled by the gag covering his mouth.

She walked next to his head and squinted at the sign taped to his feet. *Later Alligator.* She chuckled. "Herb and Shirley. Two peas from the same pod. Even joking around while they're screwing someone over."

Pulling up a straw mat, she sat and brushed his hair back. "Must keep tidy, young man." She tilted her head and laughed. "Is that a gun around your waste, or are you glad I'm here?"

She reached under his shirt and loosened his belt. "Well, well, what have we here?" She pulled the gun. "A nine millimeter." She wagged her finger at Larry. "And the safety is off. You could have blown off your nuts." She attached the safety. "I'll just hold onto this, for now."

Leona smiled. "Why, you're Larry, the day manager." She walked to his feet and pulled off the sign. "You teamed up with Herb and Shirley to rob Dirty Sam's?" She opened the stock pouch exposing the crossbow. Larry squealed. Leona smiled and pulled a Sharpie holding it up for Larry to see. She turned the note over and wrote something on the back side.

"Don't worry, Larry. Just corresponding with my friends." She put the Sharpie back. "Oh, you saw the Ravin. Not to worry. You're worth more to me now alive than dead."

She returned to his head. "Now, I'm going to remove you and take you somewhere safe. Don't fight me, young man. I have a knife and a short temper." She grabbed the handles of the dolly and lifted. She rolled the captive out of the hut.

She returned, took her new note, and attached it to the mat.

●　　　●　　　●　　　●　　　●

Herb pulled the truck into a remote area of an industrial park in Manahawkin. He jumped out and scanned for any activity. They opened the back and lifted out the money satchels. Shirley unlocked a nearby Chevy and the pair dumped the bags into the trunk. She pulled a license plate, removed the existing one, and applied a stolen tag. She stood back to admire her work. "My sister's clunker. I took it off her hands for a hundred bucks. I knew it would come in handy."

Shirley pulled the keys and the couple jumped in. It started, though belching smoke. "That will stop after a few miles, Herb." She reached for a CD and inserted one into the player. "Born to Be Wild" blared out. "Now let's free Larry. He's probably wanted in three states by now. He should at least be able to run."

●　　　●　　　●　　　●　　　●

Mark and Ted compared notes. "Well, we're looking for Larry Harkins," Mark said. "I wonder which way he went. I imagine he and his partners dumped the Brinks truck somewhere. Send the particulars to every police station in the tristate area."

"How much did Benny and Greta say they got," asked Ted.

"About two hundred and fifty grand. Not a bad day's work. I wonder what his plans are now."

"Stay low and wait, I guess," Ted said. "With his picture splattered on Facebook and later in the papers and at every police station, he'll need to find somewhere really remote."

Mark nodded. "Let's go back and think this out."

They got to the station around six. Mark started a pot of coffee, and pulled Girl Scout thin mints from his cabinet. "I guess this isn't a time for Bourbon, Ted," he said. "Have to keep our wits about us."

He swiveled his chair and watched as the local rush hour was winding down. He saw neon lettering scrolling by: *Surprise Them with Dahlias.* "Huh, Harbor Florists is closed. They normally stay open on Wednesday nights."

•   •   •   •   •

Leona stoked the campfire and rotated the squirrel. "Don't worry, Larry. They'll be back tonight. They wouldn't leave you strapped to a dolly, all alone." She laughed. "Especially with predators around."

She studied her dinner companion. "Well, I have your gun. If you promise to be good, I'll get you off of that contraption and feed you some dinner."

"Uuuunnnnfffff, uuuunnnnfffff, uuuunnnnfffff."

"I'll take that as a *yes.*" She undid the straps, removed his gag, and stood back. "Normally I'd advise my guest to not yell, as that would be impolite." She pointed the 9 mm. "Get my drift?"

Larry nodded. "Mrs. Galley, I really need to pee."

Leona tilted her head. "Remember Cool Hand Luke, Larry? Piss into that bush over there. You can stand behind for privacy, but every few seconds rattle the bush and say, "Shaking the bush, Boss."

He rubbed his shoulder. "Ok." He hurried and oohed and aaaahhhhed as he unzipped. The bush crackled as Larry mumbled "Oh, Boy." Silence.

"Larry?"

Rustling. "Shaking the bush, Boss."

He returned, relieved of his burden. Leona pointed to his pants. "Fly, Larry."

Zipping, he sat near the fire. "What now?"

Leona pushed the baked squirrel onto a bed of leaves, broke sections with a stick, and blew on it. "We have some dinner, chat awhile, and wait for our other guests." She gestured to dinner. "Dig in, Larry. You must be famished."

He stared at a drumstick.

"Oh, I forgot." She pulled bourbon and a bottle of water from her sack. "Have to wash it down with something."

A half hour later, the squirrel was consumed as was the flask of bourbon.

Larry hummed a tune. "That sounds familiar, Larry," Leona said.

"It's a song from Jaws," Larry slurred.

"I had a little drink about an hour ago," Leona joined in. "And it went straight to my head."

Headlights shone through the trees. "Shhh," Leona said. She kicked dirt onto the fire. "Our friends are arriving."

The car stopped a hundred yards from the duck blind. The couple left the car. "I smell squirrel," Herb said.

"Maybe you're just hungry," Shirley responded. "Let's let Larry go, toss him some water and tell him sayonara. She laughed. "Oh, and thanks for the money." Shirley pulled her derringer. "Let's go."

Herb pulled back the canvas door to the duck blind, switched on his flashlight, and walked in. Shirley followed, holding the gun and a bottle of water. "What the fuck?" Herb said.

No dolly, no Larry. Shirley pointed to the paper on the bamboo mat. Herb focused the light, then read the note.

"What's it say?"

Herb gritted his teeth. "*After a while Crocodile.*"

He switched off the light and signaled Shirley to follow him out. He pulled back the canvas opening. Another flashlight turned on. Leona stood next to Larry. Both grinning. "Aren't you going to invite us in?"

•　　　•　　　•　　　•　　　•

Herb and Shirley sat on the bamboo mat. Larry stood, while Leona twirled Shirley's derringer while sitting on a small cot.

"So what have you two been up to? My new friend Larry tells me you robbed Dirty Sam's." She waved her thumb at her drinking buddy. "And cleverly framed him for it."

Herb smiled. "It was almost the perfect plan. Frustrated day manager pulls off a scam while a kid's party magician holds everyone's attention, including the guards."

He turned to Leona. "We got your hundred grand. That's why we cooked this up."

The florist smiled. "I figured you were up to something. Oh well, at least it was for a good cause." She smiled. "Larry, how much do you think they pulled in?"

Larry sat next to Leona, thought a minute, and said, "I'm guessing about four hundred grand. We were really pulling it in today."

"Where's the money now, Pine," Leona said. "And don't bullshit me."

Herb sighed. "It's in the trunk."

"I saw you drive in, Shirley. Toss the keys at my feet. And no trickery. I owe your boyfriend a bullet from Baltimore. Don't make me pay up."

Shirley tossed over the keys. Leona turned to Larry and stroked his hair. "Now my friend, take the bags out of the car." She grabbed a fistful of hair. "And no tricks, Larry. I'll be watching."

Larry walked out, whistled a happy tune, and walked to the trunk. He took out the bags and returned. "Now, count it out, Larry."

•   •   •   •   •

Jim Cooper sat at the dinner table, swirled his Merlot, and drummed his fingers.

"How are you feeling, Jim? That must have been an awful experience," said Jan. "Seeing the Brinks truck almost run you over, then seeing those guards piled up in a heap."

"You know, Jan. There was something about that driver that seemed familiar. He was wearing a mask, but there was something about him. Where have I seen him before?"

"I'll put Mary Ann to bed," Jan said. "Try to relax."

Jim nodded. "Ok." He saw the newspapers and magazines stacked in the family room. "Tomorrow's trash day. I'll bind those up for recycling."

He pulled string and scissors from the kitchen drawer and knelt in front of the pile. He went through the stack, building separate heaps of papers and magazines. He read the headlines for each Long Harbor Press. *The days of our lives. Today's breaking news, destined to become next week's recycling.*

He saw last Thursday's local news section. On the front page, Herb Pine stood next to a smiling Greta Robinson. He had just won $10,000.

Hey, the driver of the getaway truck. Could it have been Herb Pine? He examined the photo. *Don't want to incriminate anyone just on a feeling. If I feel the same way tomorrow morning, I'll call the police.*

•   •   •   •   •

Sitting on the edge of the mat, Larry counted the money. When he finished, he looked at Leona. "Two hundred, forty-seven thousand, three hundred and six," he announced. "Oh, and sixty-seven cents."

Leona frowned. "I thought you said four hundred grand."

He smiled ever so slightly, then nodded to Leona. "Yeah. Seems a little light." He took his time looking in each bag, and counting. "Hey, there's just eight bags. Normally, there's a dozen."

Herb growled. "Leona, he's bullshitting you. This is all we got."

She checked the 9 mm, saw it was loaded, and removed the safety. "Somebody's lying to The Red Dahlia." She waved the gun between Larry, Herb, and Shirley. "Tell me, people, I gotta pee and I'm in no mood for further delay. What's the real total?" She smiled. "Tick, tock, tick, tock."

"Wait a minute," Herb said. "We're meeting Greta tomorrow at noon, at Louie's in Forked River. She'll tell you that Larry is lying."

"So, the night manager is in on this too," she said. "This is rich." She pulled duct tape from her bag and tossed it to Larry. "Tie up Shirley, hands and feet."

When Larry was done, she pointed to the tape. "Now toss the tape to Herb. Pine, tie up Larry." Herb obliged, also kneeing Larry in the groin. "Lying bastard."

"Hand me the tape, Pine and turn around." Herb hesitated. "Now, Pine!" Herb gave her the tape and turned. She crashed the 9mm onto his head. Herb fell over. "I'll just tie you up too, Pine." When she finished, she stood and yawned. "Get a good night's sleep, folks. I'm bunking down in the Chevy. Tomorrow, we meet with Greta and straighten this out."

CHAPTER 14

(Thursday the 23rd)

Mark bit into his Grande Scrambler. "Ummm, this is really good." He took a sip of his coffee. "Needs more sugar." He added four more packets and tried again. "Perfect."

Ted walked in and sat. "Taco Bell, Chief?"

"Eggs, cheese, peppers, tomatoes, onion," Mark said. "With the wrap and coffee, I got the basic food groups."

Ted gave a thumbs up. "That sure beats oatmeal."

Mark dried his fingers on a napkin and brought up his screen. "A message from the Manahawkin PD. They found a red truck in an industrial park. Markings say *Pinelands Medical Supply* but the VIN matches the Brinks truck. Manahawkin forensics is going over it. Our guys are on the way out." Mark balled up his wrapper and shot the mass across the room toward the wastebasket. It tumbled across the rim and landed inside. "A three-pointer from Porfino."

His desk phone rang. "Chief Porfino. How can I help you?" After a second, he signaled Ted to close the office door. "Jim, you say you might be able to identify the getaway driver. He had a mask on, but you have this feeling?"

"Ahuh." Mark pressed the Speaker button. "I'm putting you on speaker now, Jim. Ted Hanson is here also."

"Ok, Chief. Hello, Detective."

"Hello Jim. Who do you think was driving the getaway truck?"

"I hate to say it but I really think it was Herb Pine."

The men grunted as Mark opened Google maps. "Manahawkin is twenty miles from Forked River. Easy on and off of Route 9." Ted nodded. "Thanks, Jim. Look, if Pine contacts you, let us know."

Hanging up, Mark nodded to Ted. "Let's check out the truck, and then pay a visit to Forked River."

•　　　•　　　•　　　•　　　•

Greta woke up at ten. She stretched and smiled at her new wealth. *Not a bad payday at all. And Larry takes the fall. This is too good. Meet Herb and Shirley today to divvy things up, then off to my shift at Dirty Sam's.* She laughed. *Maybe I'll even pick up some overtime since Larry's gone.*

She opened her apartment door and picked up the morning paper. Hmmm, *A Heist at Dirty Sam's.* She read the article. *And I'm quoted saying they got two hundred fifty grand. My fifteen minutes of fame, I guess.*

Dressing, she folded the paper, pulled a jacket from her closet and walked out to her car. She started the Hyundai after three smoke-belching tries. *I guess I can afford a new car now. Have to be careful, though. Can't just start buying big ticket items. Not right away, anyway.*

She pulled out of the lot and headed toward Route 9 and Louie's pizza. She smiled. *Maybe I'll go for an extra slice. And a killer cannoli.*

•　　　•　　　•　　　•　　　•

Leona pulled back the opening while balancing Wawa coffee, Sizzlies, and the Manahawkin Times-Beacon. Duct tape was strewn on the mat next to Larry. She turned, pulled the 9 mm and scanned her surroundings. *Crap. I should have known Herb and Shirley could bite through the tape. Now where did they go?*

Back to Larry. She removed the tape and allowed him to stand. He stank of urine and maybe other matter. "Ok, Larry, back to the bush, you know the drill."

He stumbled out, found a sturdy black huckleberry, and relieved himself. The bush rustled. "Shaking the bush, Boss."

"Very good, Larry. Now you're in the spirit of things," Leona said, laughing.

"Herb and Shirley are gone. They left me here," he said. "Wouldn't even undo my tape."

"Finish up, Larry. I got some coffee and a nice Sizzli for you."

Larry zipped and walked back. He sat on a rock and opened the sausage, egg, and cheese, wolfing it down in large bites. He sipped the coffee. "What now, Mrs. Galley?"

Leona opened the newspaper. "You made the front page, Larry. Half the cops in the state are looking for you. It says you got away with two hundred fifty grand." She tossed the paper to him. "Not four hundred grand like you suggested. Maybe that's why our friends abandoned you. There's an honor among thieves, Larry. They don't like to be screwed over."

"So what now?" he repeated.

"I drive off, and you're free to go. Can't give you a weapon but can advise you to get out of these woods as quickly as you can." She reached into her pocket and put a twenty on a nearby log. "Stay away from the main roads. Call someone for help, if you want. Just remember, there are a lot of folks looking for you."

Leona smiled and pulled the car keys. "As for me, I'm going to Louie's in Forked River. Introducing myself to Greta, and wait for our mutual friends."

•   •   •   •   •

Mark hummed "Jersey Girl" as Bruce Springsteen crooned the Tom Waits song from his radio. Ted was indifferent at first, but soon joined Mark in the *Sha la la* chorus.

"So, do you think Herb realizes that Jim Cooper identified him?" Ted said.

"I hope not," Mark responded. "Especially for Cooper's sake."

"So, we check out the truck and then head to Forked River, and see if people can tell us where the Pine's live?"

Mark smiled. "We'll check in with the Forked River PD." He turned up the radio as the song concluded. "But first, we get a killer cheesesteak at Louie's."

•   •   •   •   •

Herb and Shirley walked out of the woods, and trudged north on Route 9. No success for Herb in thumbing a ride as drivers swerved and sped up when they saw the giant. "I got this, Herb," Shirley said as she saw a pickup approaching. She waved to the man. The driver slowed and rolled down the window as she smiled and adjusted her top. "Are you heading for Forked River, sweetie?" She nodded to Herb. "Me and my brother just have to get there."

The man opened the door. "Herbie, sit in the truck bed," Shirley said. "There's only room in the front for me and this handsome stranger."

Herb shrugged at the man. "My sister's very sociable."

Shirley smiled. "And three's a crowd, Herbie."

•   •   •   •   •

Greta checked her GPS. *A half hour away. Two hundred fifty, split three ways. Not a bad pay day. And with Larry gone, maybe I get promoted to day manager.*

She stopped in the Wawa to get coffee. A disheveled man, homeless probably, stirred sugar into a Colombian roast. *Crap, that's Larry.* She turned, walked out, and pulled away as the man placed his coffee on the counter. He saw Greta pull out.

Ah, Greta, good. The gang's all here. He saw the clock next to the cigarette rack. *Early for the rendezvous. This should be a grand old time.* He grabbed a beef jerky, broke his twenty, and walked out.

A woman carrying a squirming, crying toddler walked by, unable to open the door with her arms full. Larry stopped and opened the door for her. "Thanks," she said. "Good to see chivalry is still alive."

"Have a good day, ma'am."

"And you too." She smiled as she took in his state. "I hope things get better for you soon."

Larry smiled as he brushed wrinkles out of his shirt. "Oh, I'm sure they will, ma'am. Just have to stay the course."

•   •   •   •   •

Leona parked in the shopping plaza across from Louie's. She adjusted her rear view. *Hey, a post office, I wonder if they have those hunting stamps I've been looking for.* She looked at the 9 mm. *Can't be taking this into a post office.* She left the gun on the passenger seat, covering it with the newspaper. Seeing a Hallmark store a few doors down, she decided to buy a few cards too.

Larry walked across the lot, Louie's just a hundred yards away. He saw the Chevy. *Hey, that's the car Leona was driving.* He peeked into the passenger window. *There's the paper with the story about the heist.* He tilted his head. *Is that my picture?*

He tried the door. Unlocked. Checking for an approaching Leona, he opened the door and picked up the paper, exposing the gun. *Is that, yes, it's the 9 mm on the seat.* He picked it up and wedged it into his pants. *Now I'm ready for the meeting.*

•   •   •   •   •

Shirley whispered in the driver's ear. He smiled and pulled off Route 9, just south of Forked River. He got out and hurried to open the passenger door. Both smiled at Herb, as they headed for the woods. "We'll just be a few minutes, Big Brother," Shirley said as the couple walked off hand-in-hand.

Herb watched birds fly overhead. They lit on a utility wire and chirped. A minute later, more joined. On signal, unseen by man, they flew off. *Ah, nature. Animals in their native surroundings.* He heard footsteps. Shirley dangled keys from her finger. "Ready, Herb. I'm getting hungry for lunch."

•   •   •   •   •

Larry opened the jerky as he sat on a park bench, out of sight of Leona's car but yielding a view of Louie's. *Wow, look at all those birds. I wonder if they're here for the show.*

Shirley and Herb pulled up in front. Herb examined the hunting knife liberated from Shirley's passing boyfriend. "This could stand some cleaning, but will do in a pinch," he said. Hiding the knife under his shirt, they left the pickup.

They walked into Louie's. Shirley slid into a booth while Herb ordered a large pizza with barbeque chicken. He returned to the table with three large Cokes and glanced out the window. "Greta's coming," he said. "This will be unpleasant."

Greta pulled next to the pickup, saw her friends, and waved. She seemed to think for a second, then walked into the pizza shop. She sat next to Shirley, kissed her on the cheek, and then nodded to Herb. "Where are your cycles?" She laughed. "I guess you haven't gone back for them yet."

Shirley pointed to the pickup. "A loaner from a friend."

Herb cleared his throat. "Bad news, Greta. We were ambushed..."

Shirley tapped his shoulder as the cook smiled and put the steaming pizza on the table, sliced it into 8 pieces, and distributed plates.

The three dug in as the cook walked away, winking at Greta. Herb continued. "We were ambushed by Leona Galley. She took the money and tied us up. We got away before she came back. Larry's still there."

Greta took this in. "Let me get this straight. You were ambushed by a florist? Did she threaten you with carnations?"

"She had a gun and a crossbow. She's not the sweet lady she appears to be." Herb blew on his slice. "Plus I ran away with fifty grand of her money ten years ago. She wanted it back."

"So, that's fifty. We still have two hundred left."

Shirley shook her head. "She doesn't work that way. She took the whole amount."

Greta put down her knife and fork. "Well, isn't that just great. Can we get it back from her? Three against one after all."

Herb gritted his teeth. "It still wouldn't be a fair fight. Ever hear of the Red Dahlia?"

Greta sat back. "The Red Dahlia? Is that some sort of movie villain?"

"You have no idea, Greta," Shirley said. "You have no idea."

•   •   •   •   •

Well, well. The gang's all here, minus Leona. Larry finished the jerky and tossed the wrapper behind him.

"Young man, that's a bad example to set."

Larry turned. An elderly woman walking a toddler. "Beat it, Lady. And take your brat with you."

The woman gasped. "Young man, our crimes catch up with us. Better to seek the good, than to give bad example."

Larry stood and faced the woman. "Lady, I've had a bad day. I'm in the middle of this town without any means to get home, I need a shower, and now I'm arguing with an old bat with a runny-nosed kid."

The woman pulled mace and sprayed Larry. He dropped, moaning and covering his eyes. "And now you must curse the darkness, young man. Would have been better to light a candle."

She patted her grandson on the head. "Let's go, Billy. Let's get some ice cream." The boy kicked Larry in his groin and smiled at his grandmother. "I love you, Grandma. Can we walk tomorrow, too?"

"Of course, Billy. I'm sure the bad man won't be here then."

•   •   •   •   •

Leona put her purchases in the trunk and slid into the front seat. She squinted at the Louie's storefront. *Looks like the three thieves are having lunch. I'll join them.* She reached under the newspaper. No gun. She checked the floor and felt beneath the cushion. *Crap. Someone took it.* She holstered her Ravin and decided to walk toward Louie's. *A little bulky to bring this thing out in public, but maybe it will intimidate my colleagues.*

Midway, she saw a man receive a shot of spray in the eyes, from an elderly woman no less, and double over. *Hey, that's Larry.* She smiled. *Don't mess with old ladies, Larry.*

Hmmm. I wonder if he has the gun. She hurried away from Louie's and walked up the path to the prone day manager. Larry was sitting up, rubbing his eyes, and cursing. "Let me help you to your feet," Leona said.

Larry looked through his blur. Another old lady. He accepted her offer and flopped onto the bench. Leona took a small bottle of water from her purse. "Use this to clear your eyes."

He drenched his eyes, then recognized his Samaritan, and groaned. "Hi, Leona."

"Is that a gun in your pocket, or are you glad to see me, Larry?" She laughed at her joke. "Hand over the gun."

She accepted the weapon and removed the bullets. "Ok, here's how it's going to work. You're going into Louie's, sit with your friends, show the gun, and order them out. Walk them back here, to this bench. I'll be nearby." She patted her crossbow case. "Don't do anything brave or stupid. I can drop you before you know what hit you."

Larry reached for the gun. "There's a good boy. You know, Larry. You remind me of my nephew, Vincent Ferrante. Not too bright, but useful in his own way."

•   •   •   •   •

Larry walked down the hill, tucked the gun into his pocket, and walked into Louie's. He waved to the trio, sat next to Greta, pulled the gun, and pressed it to her ribs. He smiled to his booth mates. "Fancy seeing you here. What's for lunch?"

Greta studied the gun. "Hey, that's my nine millimeter," she said. "Shit, Larry, did you shoot Vincent Ferrante?" She turned to the couple. "And shoot at Herb?"

"Greta, we had a good thing going, even with your flirting with high rollers. Then Vincent enters the scene and you're screwing him and plotting together. That was gonna be *our* big payday. We could pull it off, let things chill awhile, then plan our future."

"Oh, Larry," Greta said. "You were sweet, but too weak in my book." She felt the 9 mm pressing her side. "Then you shoot Vincent when he can't even defend himself. You've always been a coward."

Herb waved. "Hello, where do I come in?"

"I saw her grab your ass. You turned her head. This tall, mysterious man, legendary at the tables, and according to the female employees, an animal in bed."

Herb shrugged at Shirley, who sipped her Coke and thought this over. "Ok, Larry, what next?"

"Our friend Leona wants to see us. Let's take a walk."

They stood, Herb left a nice tip, and the foursome marched out to meet The Red Dahlia.

•　　　•　　　•　　　•　　　•

"So I'm gonna get a mushroom cheesesteak, with fried onions," Mark said. "And maybe add some bacon."

"Sorta kills your diet, Chief. Doesn't it?"

Mark nodded. "I'll have to be good for a while. Maybe skip Dunkin and McDonalds for a few days, but this will be worth it."

Ted pulled into the post office parking lot and parked next to a Chevy with a bad paint job. "I need some songbird stamps. Rhonda is crazy about them."

Mark laughed. "Getting serious, Ted? Once you start buying intimate gifts like U.S. postage..."

Ted tapped Mark on the shoulder. "Look at that. There's Larry, Greta, Herb, and Shirley walking out of Louie's. They're headed to the nearby park." Ted reached for the police beacon. "Should we grab them now?"

Mark shook his head. "Let's hold off and see where this leads, Ted." He scanned the park. "You don't take a noontime stroll the day after robbing a casino."

They checked their guns, left the car, and followed at a distance.

•　　　•　　　•　　　•　　　•

"We stop here," Larry said as they reached the park bench. He waved his arm. "Take a load off." He leaned to read the placard: *Made from recycled plastic.* "I love Jersey," he said. "Landfills, casinos, and recycling plants." He laughed. "I guess we'll never run out of the need for any of them."

A young woman in ripped jeans and halter top came up to Larry. "I'll take the gun," said the woman. "The nice lady asked me to return it to her." She smiled at the three on the bench. "Don't worry, it's not loaded."

Herb started to stand. "I wouldn't do that," the woman said. "She told me that you're each within her range, whatever that means."

The woman wedged the 9 mm into her pocket and smiled. "Easiest fifty bucks I've made in a while." She turned to walk away.

"We'll take that," said Mark, walking up. "Ted, cuff the young lady to the bench over there."

Mark looked around. "Are we missing anyone?" he asked, as the arrow pierced his shoulder.

Herb, Shirley, Greta, and Larry ran as Mark fell and Ted knelt at his boss's side. He called 911 and yelled "halt" to his escaping prisoners. No response, except "cool" from the young woman.

•　　　•　　　•　　　•　　　•

Mark awoke and stared at the white ceiling. Monitors beeped nearby. "He's awake," he heard. Ted appeared overhead. "Mark, you're in Southern Ocean Hospital. You took an arrow in your shoulder."

The chief tried to lift his arm, winced, and closed his eyes. "They say it missed arteries and anything of consequence. Linda's on her way."

A nurse walked in, checked his vital signs, and positioned the bed to allow Mark to sit up. "You're lucky, Chief Porfino. That was close. An inch or two and things would have been much worse."

A man in a Louie's shirt walked in with a package. "I'll take that, thanks," Ted said, handing the man a twenty. "Keep the change."

Ted reached for the bed table, and rolled it into eating position. "Your lunch, Chief. One mushroom cheesesteak, with fried onions and bacon. One large Dr. Pepper."

Mark tried again to lift his arm. "Sorry, Mark. Let me unwrap it." Mark took a bite, moaned, and winked at Ted.

Linda hurried into the room. "Mark, are you ok?" Her husband nodded, unable to verbalize with a mouth full of grilled meat.

She saw the sandwich and soda on the table, looked at Ted, who shrugged, and smiled at Mark. "Enjoy your lunch, Mark. You earned it."

Ted explained what happened. "We have the state PD and local police looking for the suspects. The young lady is cooperating, though she appears to just be a go-between."

He turned to Mark. "We're looking for Leona Galley, too. She appears to match the girl's description, plus Harbor Florists has been closed all day, and no other archers come to mind."

"There's a report of a stolen pickup," Ted continued. "Apparently, the driver was tricked out of his keys by a hairy woman who promised to bl—" He glanced up at Linda. "Perform sexual favors. She bit him and stole the keys while he was otherwise preoccupied." Ted laughed. "He gave a statement to Lacey Township PD while icing off his co—" Ted paused again.

Linda swatted Ted's shoulder. "You can say cock. I know what they are."

"Anyway, we have all units looking for the pickup, too."

Mark licked his fingers, crumpled the wrapping paper, and pushed it aside. "Ted, call the casino..." He stopped, discovering a fried onion stranded on the plastic table. He dangled it like a collegian preparing to consume a goldfish, then dropped it into his mouth. "Tell them to look out for Pine, his girlfriend, Leona, Larry, and Greta Robinson."

•   •   •   •   •

LaVonne walked the rows of cars. *The casino still pulls them in, even after a robbery.* She saw Shirley kick starting her Harley. "Yoo hoo," she called out and walked toward her. "Did you stay overnight? Did you hear about the robbery?"

Shirley flinched as she heard LaVonne and saw her come near. "I did, LaVonne. What's happening to the world these days?" She looked at her watch. "Well, gotta go." She drove off.

Another loud rumbling, one row over. Herb Pine starting his cycle. He saw LaVonne and waved. "Have a nice day, Mr. Pine," she shouted over the roar. Herb returned a thumbs up and sped off.

LaVonne continued her rounds. A pickup, engine still warm, was parked across the painted yellow lines, taking up two spaces. *I hate when an inconsiderate person does that. The spaces are large enough.*

Her walkie-talkie beeped. She read the LEDs as they scrolled across. MANNY. "Yeah, Boss. What's up?"

She listened, then leaned against the truck. "Watch out for Herb Pine, his girlfriend, Leona, Larry, *and* Greta Robinson? They're persons of interest in the robbery?" She took a breath. "Well, actually, Herb and Shirley both took off on their Harleys about ten minutes ago." She walked toward the employee parking. "Greta's car isn't here."

•   •   •   •   •

Greta pulled into a shopping center in Barnegat. *Shit, I can't go back to my apartment, I can't go back to Dirty Sam's. The cops are probably looking for me.*

A Buick, burning oil, drove by. Black, but with patches covering body repairs. It continued past customer parking and headed toward the back of the storefronts. Greta pulled a leather case from her glove compartment, drove past the end store, and turned to the back. She saw the car, still knocking. After a minute, it let out one final rattle and quieted.

Greta checked for human activity, then removing a Philips head from the case, hurried to the back of the car, and removed the license plate. She took off her plate and fastened the other to her rear. Walking to a dumpster, she folded her old plate into quarters and flung it into the container. She rubbed her hands, got in her car, and drove away. *The cops won't find 865-LOC on the road. Now to drive to Delaware and stay low for a while.*

•   •   •   •   •

Leona drove the Chevy south on Route 9. She checked her GPS. Cape May twenty miles away. The Cape May-Lewes Ferry another five miles. A leisurely cruise across the water, then down Route 1 in Delaware, and on to Maryland. *Not my expected Thursday afternoon trip, but maybe a new beginning for The Red Dahlia, two hundred fifty grand richer.*

I'm glad I was only leasing Harbor Florists. She glanced at the photo on her console. *Shit. I forgot about Ms. Spots. She's outside, no doubt screwing some alley. Oh, well. Some kid may see her and take her in as a stray. Spots is a survivor, just like her mommy.*

She arrived at the terminus and pulled into the auto lane. A neon timetable indicated that the next crossing was an hour away. She left the Chevy and walked to the concession booth. Buying a sweet roll and large coffee, she watched the television mounted in the corner. Her face appeared. Wanted as a Person of Interest in the robbery at Dirty Sam's.

Hurrying to her car, she left the queue awaiting the ferry, put on a scarf and sunglasses, and drove off.

CHAPTER 15

(Friday the 23rd)
Evers read the Long Harbor Press: *Persons of Interest Named in Casino Robbery.*

He sipped his coffee, bit a chunk off his sweet roll and sighed. *Herb Pine, you idiot. Getting involved in a casino heist. Well, I can't protect you anymore.*

He read further. *Leona Galley. Of course. Why not screw up your life to the max? Hmmm, Larry Harkins and Greta Robinson. Geez, who wasn't involved?*

LaVonne rapped on the door, walked in and flopped into a guest chair. "Well, Dad. This is a mess. And now Lucky Roller is threatening to fire me." She slumped. "You know, I wouldn't blame them. I'm like that Joe Btfsblk character in Li'l Abner, the comic strip you used to read to me when I was a kid. I'm followed by this dark cloud all the time."

Evers walked over and sat in the chair next to her. "Now, LaVonne. These things happen." He put his arm around her shoulder. "We'll get these guys. They can't get far."

"I hope they throw them in jail for a long time," LaVonne said, sniffing.

"Oh, don't worry about justice. It will be swift and sure... I guarantee it."

•   •   •   •   •

Evers kissed LaVonne goodbye. *Poor kid. Caught up in matters way beyond her pay grade. Leona and Herb, partners in crime once more.*

He reached into the lower drawer of his desk, moved around coffee filters, cups, a flask of Wild Turkey, and found the notebook labeled: *University Memories.*

Now to revisit my undercover days. I'm glad I didn't destroy this. Though they'd have my hide for keeping it.

He pulled a burner cell from a different drawer and flipped through his notebook. *Here it is: Gladstone. Now to recall my cover story.* He walked to his door, closed, and then locked it. Opening a flask, he poured a shot into a Barney the Dinosaur cup, swirled the liquid, and downed half.

"Oh, boy," he whispered. "I handled this better in my younger days." He dialed his Maryland contact. A few rings, allowing one more sip.

"Hello," came the voice on the end. "Who is this?"

"Hi, Mr. Gladstone. I was thinking about the old university days." He studied his mug. Barney frolicking with Baby Bop and B.J. *Life so innocent. No predators.*

"Is this Evers, my star student?" The voice cleared his throat. "What are you up to lately?"

"Living in Long Harbor, New Jersey. I'm the mayor. Do you remember my classmate Leona? I'm afraid she's been bad. Took something that didn't belong to her." He took another sip. "I think she's coming home to Maryland, maybe even to hide on campus."

"I'll keep an eye out, Evers. Should I have security detain her?"

"That would be great. She needs to understand the consequences of her actions. I'll stop by later to greet her myself."

"Good. I'll make us a lunch. Is two okay?"

•   •   •   •   •

Herb and Shirley drove into the woods, found their cache of money and fake IDs, and sped deeper into the brush until they found a paved road used by emergency crews to fight Pineland fires. They stopped and considered their next action. "They'll be looking for the cycles. We need to ditch these, grab a car, and head to our next home," Herb said. "I have friends in Maryland I can contact."

Shirley patted her Harley. "I'm gonna miss my ride."

"There'll be other days and other Harleys, Shirley. The first order of business is to lay low until things cool off." Herb opened his satchel. "There's plenty of places to hide in Maryland. We'll plan our future, and hopefully, figure out how to get revenge on Leona."

He grinned. "Now *she* owes *me* money, and she's gonna pay up."

They crept along, trying to minimize any noise. Reaching a junction with a state road, Herb pointed to a tavern nearby and the couple parked their bikes. They walked to the gravel lot and peeked into the windows of the parked cars.

Herb grunted. No keys in any ignition. *Doesn't anyone trust their neighbor anymore?* Spotting a Toyota Camry with the keys poking out from the driver's visor, he waved Shirley over. They climbed in and drove off. A mile later, they saw a car abandoned on the side of the road. Shirley got out, opened her Swiss Army Knife, removed the license plate, switched it with the Toyota, and climbed back in. Herb smiled. "Now on to Maryland."

•   •   •   •   •

Larry walked through the woods, near Route 9, avoiding human contact. *Jeez. Yesterday, I was managing a casino, today I'm an escapee hiding from people, and down to my last ten dollars.* He heard rusting, a wolf nosing through a trash can in a pullover yards ahead. He inched forward, then tripped in a shallow hole. He fell to one knee as the wolf took notice.

He stood and limped away. The wolf left the trash can and squealed as he approached Larry. *Shit.* He hobbled toward the road. The wolf followed, then stopped as a bright light framed Larry. A car screeched to a halt.

Larry limped to the driver's side. "I have to get out of here," he told the driver. He reached into his pocket. "I'll give you ten bucks to take me to the next town."

"Get in," the man replied.

Larry slid into the passenger seat. "Thanks a lot," he said, holding the ten toward the man.

"Keep it, Harkins." The man smiled, and put the police beacon onto his roof. "We were covering this road waiting for you. I win the lottery. Two hundred bucks on who lands you first." He smiled. "Maybe I'll hit Dirty Sam's later on and see if I can turn it into a grand."

•   •   •   •   •

Ted walked into Mark's office. "They got Larry Harkins. Maybe we can clear this up and recover the money before the state brass get here and kicks our ass."

Mark crushed his Burger King bag. "Did they find any money on him?"

"Ten bucks. He says Leona has it all."

Mark spun around and studied Harbor Florists. "Still closed. And probably not reopening under the same management. Leona's priority number one now, then Herb, Shirley, and Greta." He squinted at the neon marquee. "And get someone to turn off that damn dahlia message."

CHAPTER 16

Leona drove into a Valero station near Elkton Maryland. She sat at the pump and looked into the mini-mart. Another car pulled up. A man left the driver's side, pulled the pump, and started fueling.

Crap, they have self-service here. Jersey spoiled me. She left the Chevy and circled the car. "Can I help you, ma'am?" the man called over.

"My daughter's car. Now where is that fuel door?"

He walked over and gestured to the front driver side door. "You should have a gas latch. Do you mind?" he asked.

Leona nodded. The man leaned inside, pulled the latch, and the fuel door opened. He walked around the Chevy. "It's on the passenger side, ma'am. Not sure why they put it there."

She smiled and nodded. "Thanks, young man. I got it from here."

He saluted and walked into the mini-mart. He started to pour coffee when a state trooper walked over. "Hey, Charlie. Helping an old lady. Very nice."

"My good deed for the day, Mike" he said. "Such a nice lady." He shook his head. "Must be a hunter. She's got a crossbow case in the back."

• • • • •

Herb pulled the Toyota into a Citgo off Route 40 in Havre De Grace. "Forty miles or so to Baltimore. I wonder if my former associates are still around," he said to Shirley.

"Let's hope so," she said. "Just be careful, Herb. You don't know who you can trust these days." She left the car and walked to the mini mart.

Herb flipped through the contacts list on his smartphone as the car filled with Regular. "Ah, Mr. Gladstone, my former contact. He's getting along now, but may still be useful."

He entered the number, hit the green dial button, leaned against the hood and whistled. An answer, then, "Who is this?"

"Mr. Gladstone remember me. Herb Pine, your student from university?"

Silence. "Hi, Pine. What's up?"

Herb thought a moment. "I was in the area and wanted to stop by. Rehash old times, maybe spend a few days."

"So what have you been doing all these years, Pine? Haven't seen you in ten years or so."

"Oh, hunting, fishing, giving tours of the Jersey Pinelands," he said. "And hitting the casino in Long Harbor when I need a few extra bucks. Anyway, me and my girl decided to take off and see this great land. First stop: Baltimore: Birthplace of the Star-Spangled Banner."

A pause. "Ok, Pine. You can stop by. Remember my place on Light Street. Come by around two. We'll go over old times."

"See you then. Thanks, Mr. Gladstone."

Gladstone hung up and stared at his smartphone. *Same shit, different day. Evers and Herb at the same time, maybe even Leona, if Evers is right.* He walked to his greenhouse. "Must put out some fresh flowers," he whispered. "Maybe not red dahlias."

Shirley came out of the mart. "Any luck with your associates," she said as she handed Herb a Devil Dog and a Mountain Dew.

Herb tore open the wrapper and took a large bite. He took a swig from the soda, swirled to loosen any chocolate from his teeth, and swallowed. "Aaaahhhh. This hits the spot." He put the gas pump back in place. "I found an old Baltimore associate. We'll pay him a visit around two." He pulled a twenty and walked toward the mart. "It's good to be back in town."

Shirley sat in the passenger seat and checked her smartphone. *Crap, Herb's picture is plastered all over the news. Lucky, they don't have one of me.* "Herb," she called out. Her boyfriend stopped and spread his hands in a "what's up" gesture. She waved him over and held up her phone. "You're on the front page. Let me pay for the gas. Just be ready to go when I get back."

Herb sat in the passenger seat and guzzled the Mountain Dew. He found CDs in the glove compartment and placed a Springsteen into the player. He slid low to avoid passing motorists as Shirley returned.

"I bought a few lottery tickets. Might be our next best chance at a big payday." She stroked her stomach. "In the meantime, I'm starving. You might be able to last on Devil Dogs, but I need some red meat. Something that once roamed the earth."

She nodded to the highway. "There's an Arby's. I'll get us something and we'll pull off and have lunch. We have some time until our meeting at two."

●　　　●　　　●　　　●　　　●

Greta drove into Rehoboth, found a parking space near the bandstand and collected her thoughts. A knock on the window. "Gotta feed the meter, ma'am," said a uniformed woman wearing a City of Rehoboth shirt. Greta smiled and nodded. She left the car, slid three quarters into the meter, and stood quietly, watching the tide come in and out.

Putting on sunglasses, she pulled a Predators cap from her glove compartment and walked toward Grotto's Pizza. She sat as a table in the back, ordered two slices of mushroom and a Diet Pepsi and watched the TV monitor. The noon news was on, a man in a bad toupee read the breaking stories.

Her photo came up on the screen. *Crap.* The waitress returned and placed the pizza and soda in front of her. She started to glance at the monitor, Greta put her hand on the waitress's arm. "Can you bring me an order of cheesy bread?"

The waitress smiled and walked back to the kitchen. Greta's picture on the newscast was replaced by a map of the Atlantic coast. A shapely meteorologist told of a coming storm. *Gotta get out of town in a little while. At least until the story and the storm blow over.*

Walking outside, she sat at a bench and closed her eyes, listening to the ocean churn, anticipating rough weather. *How long do I have to run?*

"Please, stand, Miss. Arms behind your back." Greta turned. A Delaware state trooper. "I'm taking you in. You're wanted in New Jersey for Grand Theft."

•　　•　　•　　•　　•

Ted walked into Mark's office. "They arrested Greta Robinson in Rehoboth, Delaware. Identified by a meter maid."

Mark put an X next to Greta's casino picture. "Ok, great. Put in the extradition paperwork."

He looked over the three remaining APBs. "We're down to Leona, Herb, and Shirley," he said. "Let's hope we get them without further trouble."

•　　•　　•　　•　　•

Evers told Susie he would be out for the day. He set his GPS for Light Street, Baltimore and turned into the afternoon traffic. He found a smooth jazz CD and slid it into the player. *OK, Kenny G, calm me down. I* need to be rational when I confront Leona. Maybe we can work something out that spares any pain, lets LaVonne keep her job, and recovers the money.

He crossed into Pennsylvania and found his way onto I-95. *Damn, traffic is slowing down already. Probably some idiot who just had to dodge in and out of lanes.* He read the dashboard clock. *I won't make it for two o'clock. That's a shame. I hope he holds lunch.*

He got off at Havre De Grace and fueled up as he took in the busy crossroads. "An Arby's," he whispered. "Not on my diet, but I'm hungry and away from LaVonne." He drove into the lot as a Toyota pulled out, the two occupants heading south on Route 40. A wrapper flew out the window. Evers walked over, retrieved the wrapper, and tossed it into a waste can. *Litterers. I hope someone catches you the next time.*

•   •   •   •   •

Leona reached the Baltimore city limits. She pulled off I-95, found a 7-Eleven and parked. She checked the newsfeed on her phone. *Damn, Larry and Greta both arrested. They're looking for me, Herb, and Shirley. I'll have to find somewhere to lay low for a few days. Lucky for me, I have some packaged snacks and water in my trunk.* She reached into the back seat. *And my trusty Ravin.*

She headed east, looking for a campground. She saw a motel. DAY RATES it announced. *Hmmm. The place needs some serious maintenance, but it will do for now.* She saw a large house a hundred yards away, sharing a driveway with the lodging. *Oh, boy. Looks like the Bates Motel.* She adjusted her scarf and sunglasses after parking near the door, and went inside.

A woman came out of a back office. "Hello, dearie. Do you need a room?" She leaned forward on the counter and studied her car. "Only for one? OK. I guess you want a full day. Forty dollars."

Leona pulled money from her purse as the woman pushed the registry in front of her and handed her a pen. "Just one night," Leona said.

"There's a Denny's down the road if you're hungry." She opened a mini fridge. "Got a few Buds, and jerky if you don't want to make the trip."

"I'll take a beer," Leona said. "I just need some peace and quiet." She filled out the registry entry.

"Ok, Ms. Dahlia," the woman said. "Here's your key, number two, right next to the office."

"Do you have anything out back?"

The woman turned to the key rack. "There's number twelve." She smiled. "Have to warn you, it gets pretty lonely back there. And wild animals may wander by."

"I hope so," Leona said. "I love wild animals."

Leona drove off. "What a nice lady," the woman whispered as the TV screen in the back room switched from the casino robbery to high school football.

•　　　•　　　•　　　•　　　•

Gladstone poured Cognac into a crystal decanter, checked each glass for smudges, pulled Cuban cigars from a drawer, and hurried into the kitchen to check on the scones. *I have to admit, this is exciting. Visits from old friends, who will no doubt attack each other on sight.*

He looked out his picture window. *Light Street. Now filled with skyscrapers, busy commuters, and mostly law abiding citizens. Oh, for the old days where people would slit your throat on a whim, or better yet, steal your fortune, one scam at a time.*

And Herb Pine is back. Always living on the edge of the law, but valuable enough to my employers to have that ignored. Gladstone smiled and poured a shot of VSOP. *And now he's running from something. Except he left enough of a trail to need refuge.*

He sat, smiled, and lit a cigar. *And just his luck to get in trouble close to Evers Wilson. What are the odds? Well, Herb may still be useful to the Baltimore office. I'll have to see how this plays out. Evers is a good friend, but he's pragmatic enough to see beyond petty crime.* He blew smoke rings toward the yellowed ceiling and glanced at the grandfather clock. *One-thirty, tick tock, Herb. I can't wait.*

•   •   •   •   •

Leona bit into the squirrel drumstick. *Not bad. The Maryland wildlife always tastes different.* She checked her watch and gulped the Bud. *One-thirty. I wonder if my Baltimore contacts are back from their lunch.* She laughed. *No squirrel for them. Fancy sandwiches and bottled water, I would think. Not a predator in the bunch.*

And most of them are gone, anyway. Chased out of town by a mole who exposed them. I always suspected Pine, just couldn't prove it. And then the bastard left town owing me fifty grand. She patted the leather bags laying on the sticky, cushioned chair. *Paid in full, Pine.* She guzzled the remaining beer. *May our paths never meet again.*

She leafed through her address book. *Darnel, my muscle, co-conspirator, and Baltimore street connection. I wonder if he's still around.* She found his number and pressed the Call button.

A ring tone came from Gladstone's desk drawer. He walked over and found the chiming cell from the twenty he kept hidden away. *Darnel, huh. Who's calling his business phone?* He didn't recognize the caller number. *Have to let it go. Maybe they'll leave a voice message.*

Leona disconnected when a voice prompt came on. *Darnel was never without his phone. What's going on?* She searched her contact list again. *Miriam. Not as trustworthy as Darnel, but she'll have to do.* She pressed Call.

Another cell buzzed. Gladstone found the right one. *Miriam Quigley. Boy, this is odd. Who's calling my contacts after all these years?* He signed onto his laptop and opened a spreadsheet. *Darnel and Miriam, who do you have in common? Well, well, Leona Galley, The Red Dahlia.*

•　　　•　　　•　　　•　　　•

Herb and Shirley drove into town, navigated the traffic to Light Street, and stopped at a red light. "Wow, Baltimore is getting more built up all the time," Herb said. "Residences are yielding to skyscrapers, and it looks like a more upscale clientele." He looked at the pleather bench seats of his current ride. "No place for a beat up Toyota."

At the green light, Herb moved forward, looking for Gladstone's row house. A police car sat at the corner across from the home. Shirley tugged on Herb's shirt and pointed.

"Ok, there's an alley in the back, I'll pull into there," Herb said. "We'll knock on Gladstone's back door."

Gladstone heard a tapping in the kitchen. He lowered the sound on Sports Center and pulled his gun. He nodded and smiled as his former student stood at the back door. He undid four vertical locks and opened the steel reinforced door. "Herb Pine, long time, no see."

He turned to the hairy female beside Herb. "And this must be your girlfriend." He reached out a hand. "Just call me Gladstone." He summoned them both. Please come in and relax from your drive." He chuckled. "Mi casa, su casa."

They entered but hesitated to join him in the study. "Oh, my bad." He closed the blinds, lit a tableside lamp and pointed to the couch. "Now, how about some Cognac."

He poured as the couple seemed to unwind. "I have some Cubans also." He smiled at Herb. "I remember you were partial to them."

Shirley sat forward. "I'll take one," she said. "Been living on cheap cigars lately. Could stand a quality smoke."

Gladstone smiled, pulled one from a humidor, trimmed the end, and handed it to his new acquaintance. He flashed a personalized lighter (just a G etched into the silver), waited for Shirley to sniff the wrapped leaves, and then bite down. The lighter exposed a flame close enough to allow combustion. Shirley inhaled, pulling the flame into the cigar.

"You've done this before, Shirley, well done."

Gladstone sat back, pleased but surprised and somewhat turned on by this mysterious creature. "So, how long will you two be in town?"

"Well..." Herb started. A chime from within the house.

"Ah, my scones," Gladstone said. "Let me bring those in." He hurried to the kitchen. "Ah, these are perfect."

After a minute, he returned with a tray of steaming pastries. He waved his oven mitt, attempting to cool them off.

He glanced up as he placed the tray on the table. "So, you were saying, Herb, how long you'd be in town." Herb leaned forward and sniffed the scones.

"They're cranberry, Pine. Harvested at their ripest."

Herb picked one up and took a large bite. "Ummmm," He held up one finger. "I'm tasting orange, too."

Gladstone smiled. "Very good catch. Just enough to lessen the full impact of the berries."

Shirley put her cigar in an antique ash tray and sat forward. "Mr. Gladstone, Herb and I will be in town a few days before we head off." Herb licked his fingers and wiped them on the linen napkin. "We were hoping we could stay here a few days, to get our bearings and decide where to go next."

Gladstone waved his arms, indicating a panorama of the room. "Shirley, as I said before 'Mi casa, su casa.'" He stood. "I have a lovely bedroom overlooking the harbor. Why don't you two take that room? You're welcome to stay as long as you need."

The pair smiled and rose. "We'll unpack a few things," Herb said. "Then, if you don't mind, we're a bit grimy from the road. We'd like to shower and change."

"Of course, you two. There're towels and robes in the closet. Take your time, do your ablutions, and come down. I'll scare up a late lunch."

Herb and Shirley returned from the Toyota. Gladstone walked them up the winding staircase and opened the door to a large bedroom, well-furnished, and overlooking the harbor. "Take your time, settle in, and come down when you're ready. Does a nice goulash sound good?" He laughed, anticipating Herb's question. "No squirrel, I'm afraid, but some nice beef, fresh from the market."

●   ●   ●   ●   ●

Herb walked out of the bathroom, toweling off every nook and cranny. He fastened his robe. Shirley sat in a lounger, head wrapped in a towel and reading *Zen and the Art of Motorcycle Maintenance*.

Herb read the cover and smiled. "Not a guide to how to fix your Harley, Shirley," he said. "But good advice on how to transform your life."

Shirley marked her place with a piece of writing paper and grabbed Herb by the lapels. "Transform me here, Herb Pine," she said.

The couple embraced, moving like a blue crab to the safe harbor of the king-sized bed, and forgot about Dirty Sam's, Leona, and life on the run.

●   ●   ●   ●   ●

Herb rolled off Shirley and sighed.

"Gladstone must have a lot of money," Shirley said as she stroked his hair.

"I think he was born to wealth," Herb said. "But pretty sharp, and able to make a good living."

"What's he do?" she asked.

"He deals in human beings, information, the occasional double-dealing, and services to parties on both sides of the law."

Shirley sniffed the air. "That smells like the goulash. I'm starving.

Ready to go down, Herb?"

Herb nodded. The couple washed up, dressed in clean clothes, and walked downstairs. As they turned the corner into the dining room, they saw another guest. They stopped and turned toward the back door. Evers raised his gun. "Please join us, you two. There's plenty for us all."

●　　●　　●　　●　　●

Leona turned onto Lombard, headed to Little Italy. *I need a large glass of Chianti. Have to see who else I can contact now that Darnel and Miriam don't appear to be around.* She tried them both again. No answer.

She scrolled through her contact list and sipped her wine. She put down her phone and scooped bruschetta onto a piece of bread. She swiped an olive-oil-coated finger over her screen.

Godfrey Churchill, she read. *I wonder if he is still in the business. Has that brownstone on Light Street. A bit stuffy for me, but, as I recall, someone always willing to lend a hand.*

She called his number. Gladstone recognized the tone coming from his desk drawer. "Excuse me a minute folks," he said to his guests. "Evers, I trust you can lead the conversation while I check on who's calling." Evers nodded.

He walked into his study, opened the desk drawer, and checked the calling number. He turned to his spreadsheet after dismissing his Buckingham Palace screensaver. "Well, well, Leona Galley, The Red Dahlia," he whispered. "Now we have a real party."

He checked his alias for Leona and returned the call. "Leona Galley. Godfrey Churchill here. I *just missed* answering before the ringing stopped."

Leona took a sip of her wine. "Godfrey. Good to hear your voice. I was in town and wondered if I could stop by."

"That would be lovely, Leona. Do you remember where I am on Light Street? I'm cooking up some goulash, so I hope you're hungry.

As I recall, you were also partial to Chianti. I'll open a fresh bottle."

"Wonderful," Leona said. "I should be there in a few minutes. It will be nice to reminisce about the past."

"I'll leave the light on, Leona. So good to hear from you."

Gladstone disconnected and smiled. *What a fun day this has been.*

He returned to the dining room. His three guests were digging into the goulash, with Shirley also hitting the wine pretty well.

"Herb, Shirley, Evers. Guess who's coming to dinner?"

•   •   •   •   •

Mark and Ted sat in Mark's office and wolfed down Wawa hoagies. Mark struggled with a Tastykake wrapper as Ted finished his Dr. Pepper, then patted his stomach. "Man, Mark. I must have put on five pounds since the robbery."

The Chief nodded. "Yeah, Ted. Sorry. I know we've been putting in crazy hours, but this looks bad for our PD and we need to get this cleared up before the state decides to take the investigation over."

"How could Herb, Shirley, and Leona have just disappeared?" Ted said. Wonder if they're still in Jersey."

"Could be anywhere on the east coast, maybe even gone west. We have APBs out, but we're not even sure what they're driving. State troopers recovered their motorcycles, but they apparently stole a Toyota nearby. No match yet on the plates. Leona's car was found in the woods. Tracks from another car were nearby. We're trying to identify those now."

Mark dialed a number, then hung up after a few rings. "Evers seems to be out. At least *he's* not breathing down our necks."

•   •   •   •   •

Leona pulled onto Light Street and stopped a block from Godfrey's brownstone. She reached for her box of English toffee and decided to walk the rest of the way. She stopped and thought. *He seemed almost too cordial after ten years. Can't let my guard down.* She returned to the Chevy, put the Ravin into the front seat, and scanned for a different approach to the house. *Maybe there's a back way in.*

She found the alley and parked next to a Toyota with New Jersey tags. Opening the leather case, she checked her weapon. *Ready to go.* She put it on the floor to be out of sight, and picking up the box of toffee, approached the rear of the house.

From the back window she saw lights on and heard conversation. She ducked and worked her way along the side of the house. Louder talk and a familiar voice. She raised herself to eye level and peeked into a window. Evers was talking to Herb and Shirley.

"Leona. You don't have to skulk around," Godfrey said pointing his gun. "I think you know my company already. Let's go in and join them."

Leona walked into the open kitchen. He closed the door, then motioned her into the dining room.

Evers stopped talking while Herb and Shirley turned at the footsteps approaching. "Gentlemen, and lady, we have an additional guest. Leona, just sit next to Shirley. I'll set another place."

He took the yellow box from Leona as she sat. "Oh my, you brought toffee. My favorite."

●　　　●　　　●　　　●　　　●

"Well, aren't we a rogues gallery," He said as he laid out a plate and silverware in front of Leona. He ladled goulash as Evers stood sentry.

"In case there's some name confusion, I go by Godfrey Churchill Gladstone. Evers and I worked for the same benefactor. Over the years, I had the pleasure of conducting business with Herb, who was also briefly in my employ, and Leona who provided me with business solutions not normally advertised. Evers, you hadn't actually met Leona in person before but apparently you're acquainted now."

He nodded to Leona's plate. "Please, my dear. You must be famished." He nodded to Herb. "Please fill Leona's glass. She's partial to Chianti."

Godfrey stabbed the last chunk of beef on his plate and downed it. "Wow, I've really outdone myself," he said. He pulled his gun again. "Evers, dig in. I'll take guard duty."

He sipped his wine and studied his guests. "Here's what's going to happen. Leona, I assume the money is still in your car. A beat up Chevy from what I see. Please surrender your keys. I'll have an associate fetch the bags, and, if I know you, disarm the crossbow." Leona tossed over the keys as the back door opened.

He turned to Herb and Shirley. "Evers tells me that your little robbery cast poor LaVonne into a bad light. She may lose her job." He took another sip. "We can't have that."

A hulking man walked in. Gladstone pushed over the keys. "Rusting red Chevy out back, Freddie. Money bags, probably in the trunk, and a crossbow nearby. Bring it all in." The man nodded and left. Godfrey smiled. "I feel like Solomon. How to divide up the baby and make everyone happy."

• • • • •

"Two hundred, forty-seven thousand, three hundred and six," Freddie said. "Oh, and sixty-seven cents."

Gladstone smiled. "So, Herb, you stiffed Leona for fifty grand if I remember ancient history. A Ravin runs around two grand, loss of business, blah, blah, blah. Leona, you get sixty thousand."

He turned to the couple. "Herb and Shirley, you had the wherewithal to pull off the robbery, but you lost your home." Godfrey laughed. "—and standing in the community. You get twenty grand together."

He watched with pride as Freddie attacked a plate of goulash. "I'm not greedy. I'll take the forty-seven grand for my trouble, and to compensate my associate here." Freddie smiled through missing teeth.

"Evers, that leaves a hundred and twenty grand. Nice compensation for you and your lovely daughter. Let things chill, then give her a nice share." He puffed on his cigar.

"It's probably better if they fire her anyway," he said, nodding to Herb and Shirley. "You meet such unsavory characters there."

Freddie reached into his coat pocket and pulled cloths.

"Now, my associate here will put you to sleep, drive you to the woods, and let each of you go. Don't bother struggling. You'll awaken from the chloroform, probably not from a bullet." He finished the last few bites of his meal. "And don't bother coming back here. You won't leave alive."

He waved to his associate. "Freddie, do the honors."

●　　●　　●　　●　　●

Leona awoke, lying in a bed of leaves, covered with a blanket. A saddlebag lay next to her. She stood, found a stump, and sat. Opening the bag, she saw packets of cash, banded with the Dirty Sam's logo. She looked around. *Don't recognize this place.*

She brushed dirt from her blouse and skirt, then felt an object in her pocket. A Bowie knife, sheathed. She also found matches. *Well, at least Godfrey gives a girl a fighting chance.*

She started to count the money in the bag, but decided to wait for a better time. A small yellow packet caught her eye. *Toffee.* She laughed. *A gentleman to the end.* She unrolled a candy and let one melt in her parched mouth. A noise nearby. *One of God's creatures?*

Drawing the knife, she edged toward a tree. Behind it, a squirrel noshed on an acorn unaware of its fate. The knife plunged into its back. *Now for some breakfast, then I make my way out of here.*

•   •   •   •   •

Herb and Shirley found a country road about half a mile from their drop off point. Walking due south, they found a diner. Ordering stacks of pancakes, they downed coffee and read the placemat identifying local businesses. "I think we're on the Eastern Shore," Shirley said.

A car pulled up, farting and coughing. A woman in a waitress uniform climbed out, pushed against the driver side door, apparently to make sure it closed, and came in. A few minutes later, she walked to the table. "I'm Lorrie. Your waitress is on break. Do you need anything?"

Herb grinned, showing syrup coated teeth. "We saw you drive in. Got car problems?"

"What a heap," she said. For ten bucks, I'd leave it there for the next lucky owner."

Shirley smiled and reached into the bag. She counted off three hundred. "You're in luck. We just happen to need a car."

•   •   •   •   •

"LaVonne, we have to let you go," Manny said. "Corporate is getting a lot of heat from Dirty Sam's over the robbery. They need a fall guy. It was your shift, so you're it." He opened a drawer. "Lucky Roller is giving you five hundred for severance. Sorry to see you go."

LaVonne drove off to City Hall and cried when she met her father. "Don't worry, honey. Things will work out," he said. "Why don't you sign up for the next semester of community college? Maybe take up cosmetology like you always wanted. I'll front you the tuition."

He smiled as he hugged her. "And if you get good grades, we'll get you a decent car."

LaVonne stopped crying and smiled. "You see, little girl. Things work out eventually."

CHAPTER 17

(Three Months Later)

Mark sipped his decaf and spooned his oatmeal. *This really sucks.* He checked his stomach per his daily routine. *I have to admit, I do feel better after losing twenty pounds. And I can fit into my old suits now.*

Ted walked in, nodded, gestured to Mark's breakfast, and continued over to the window, taking in the landscape. "Indian summer, Mark. The leaves are starting to fall. But still time to get to the beach. Rhonda and I rented a house for a week. Would you and Linda care to join us?"

Mark spun his chair around. "I guess we're both due some time off after we finished the Dirty Sam's investigation." He looked out at Bay Florists, formerly Harbor Florists. Mrs. Turner, the owner, swept the sidewalk and, noticing Mark and Ted, waved.

"I can't believe they vanished into thin air," Ted said. A few moments of silence. "At least we found out who killed Vincent Ferrante. Larry confessed and his prints were all over the gun."

Mark nodded. "And one of the money bags turned up. Blocks from the casino. Must have fallen out, somehow."

He tossed his decaf into the trash can, opened his desk, and removed a Ring Ding. "It didn't yield any evidence. The casino was happy to get it back, though." He unwrapped the snack and took a long, sensuous sniff, which slightly unnerved Ted. "Benny Watson, the general manager, told me the recovered cash would cover the increased insurance premiums. So the casino doesn't lose a thing."

"I guess, as they say, the house always wins," said Ted. He read aloud the neon banner scrolling in the flower shop window: *Say It with Flowers*. "Better than *Surprise Them with Dahlias*, I guess."

•   •   •   •   •

A motorcycle rumbled down the street and the driver pulled into Mayor Evers Wilson's reserved spot. LaVonne cut the engine, removed her helmet, turned, and smiled to her father. Evers loosened his grip on her midsection and slid off the rear seat, grabbing the support bar to avoid a fall to the sidewalk.

"LaVonne, I promised you a car, not a Harley. Are you sure this is what you want?"

His daughter smiled. "This is perfect, Dad. I feel like a kid again."

She nodded across the street to Bay Florists. "You know, Dad. It's not too late to start over, yourself."

Evers kissed her on the cheek, staggered slightly to the door of the City Hall/Police Station, turned, and waved as LaVonne drove away.

Mrs. Turner, new owner of Bay Florists, smiled at Evers as she finished sweeping the sidewalk in front of her shop. "Good morning, Mr. Mayor. Beautiful day isn't it?"

He smiled. "That it is, Mrs. Turner." He took a deep breath and crossed the street. "Would you like to meet for lunch?"

•   •   •   •   •

A heavyset, red-bearded man walked into a Kentucky sporting goods store, approached the counter, and pointed to the Ravin R15 mounted on the wall. "Can I see one of the salesmen about the Ravin," he said to the woman spraying Windex onto the glass countertop.

"I can help you, sir," Leona said. "That's a fine piece of hunting gear. My own personal preference. Can split the skull of small game, or bring down larger prey."

The man was silent.

"Not expecting such a response from an old woman? I assure you sir, I could circumcise you from a hundred feet with one of the bolts."

The man nodded and edged toward the door. "Thanks ma'am. I think I'll just be going now."

"A-hole," Leona muttered. "He'll be prey before he's ever a predator."

•   •   •   •   •

A tall, dark, clean-shaven man walked into the Mississippi casino, found a blackjack table with an empty chair and sat. He winced. *Shaving off all my body hair was uncomfortable. I still bleed from the hard-to-get-at areas. Oh, well. Phillip Baxter is a new man. So long, Herb Pine.*

A brunette hostess came over. "Anything to drink, sir?" asked Roseanne, formerly Shirley.

"I'll have Sex on the Beach," Phillip responded, winking at the hostess.

Roseanne smiled and wrote the order. "Are you sure you can handle it, sir? It's pretty strong."

The dealer laughed, then pretended to count chips when Phillip turned to face him. He turned back to Roseanne. "Come to think of it. Make it a Bud."

Roseanne walked off. Philip bet $50 and glanced around as the cards were dealt to the players. "A nice little place," he said to the woman sitting next to him. "I'm new to the area. How's the night life?"

Her diamond bracelet reflected the bright lights. She pulled $500 from her purse and signaled the dealer for more chips.

She studied her cards, then glanced up at her table mate. "You playin' or gassin' around, buddy," she said. "I'm here to win some money." She looked him over. "We can meet for a drink later, if you're so inclined. We can talk about what the night might have to offer."

Philip glanced at his blackjack hand: a King and a Queen. "I'd like that, ma'am. I think I might just fit in fine here."

View other Black Rose Writing titles at www.blackrosewriting.com/books and use promo code **PRINT** to receive a **20% discount** when purchasing.

BLACK✿ROSE
writing™